THE GUNS OF LIVINGSTON FROST

TWO SHORT NOVELS

Borgo Press Books by ARDATH MAYHAR

The Absolutely Perfect Horse: A Novel of East Texas (with Marylois Dunn) * *The Body in the Swamp: A Washington Shipp Mystery* [Wash Shipp #2] * *Carrots and Miggle: A Novel of East Texas* * *The Clarrington Heritage: A Gothic Tale of Terror* * *Closely Knit in Scarlatt: A Novel of Suspense* * *Crazy Quilt: The Best Short Stories of Ardath Mayhar* * *Deadly Memoir: A Novel of Suspense* * *Death in the Square: A Washington Shipp Mystery* [Wash Shipp #1] * *The Door in the Hill: A Tale of the Turnipins* * *The Dropouts: A Tale of Growing Up in East Texas* * *The Exiles of Damaria: A Novel of Fantasy* * *Feud at Sweetwater Creek: A Novel of the Old West* * *The Fugitives: A Tale of Prehistoric Times* * *The Guns of Livingston Frost: Two Short Novels* [Wash Shipp #3] * *The Heirs of Three Oaks: A Novel of the Old West* * *High Mountain Winter: A Novel of the Old West* * *How the Gods Wove in Kyrannon: Tales of the Triple Moons* * *Hunters of the Plains: A Novel of Prehistoric America* * *Island in the Lake: A Novel of Native America* * *Khi to Freedom: A Science Fiction Novel* * *The Lintons of Skillet Bend: A Novel of East Texas* * *Lone Runner: A Novel of the Old West* * *Lords of the Triple Moons: A Science Fantasy Novel: Tales of the Triple Moons* * *The Loquat Eyes: More Tall Tales from Cotton County, Texas* * *Makra Choria: A Novel of High Fantasy* * *Medicine Dream: Being the Further Adventures of Burr Henderson* * *Messengers in White: A Science Fantasy Novel* * *The Methodist Bobcat and Other Tales* * *Monkey Station: A Novel of the Future* (Macaque Cycle #1; with Ron Fortier) * *People of the Mesa: A Novel of Native America* * *A Planet Called Heaven: A Science Fiction Novel* * *Prescription for Danger: A Novel of the Old West* * *Reflections; & Journey to an Ending: Collected Poems* * *A Road of Stars: A Fantasy of Life, Death, Love, and Art* * *Runes of the Lyre: A Science Fantasy Novel* * *The Saga of Grittel Sundotha: A Science Fantasy Novel* * *The Seekers of Shar-Nuhn: Tales of the Triple Moons* * *Shock Treatment: An Account of Granary's War: A Science Fiction Novel* * *Slewfoot Sally and the Flying Mule: Tall Tales from Cotton County, Texas* * *Soul-Singer of Tyrnos: A Fantasy Novel* * *Strange Doin's in the Pine Hills: Stories of Fantasy and Mystery in East Texas* * *Strange View from a Skewed Orbit: An Oddball Memoir* * *Through a Stone Wall: Lessons from Thirty Years of Writing* * *Timber Pirates: A Novel of East Texas* (with Marylois Dunn) * *Towers of the Earth: A Novel of Native America* * *Trail of the Seahawks: A Novel of the Future* (Macaque Cycle #2; with R. Fortier) * *The Tulpa: A Novel of Fantasy* * *Two-Moons and the Black Tower: A Novel of Fantasy* * *Vendetta: A Novel of the Old West* * *Warlock's Gift: Tales of the Triple Moons* * *The World Ends in Hickory Hollow: A Novel of the Future* * *A World of Weirdities: Tales to Shiver By*

THE GUNS OF LIVINGSTON FROST

TWO SHORT NOVELS

by

Ardath Mayhar

THE BORGO PRESS

An Imprint of Wildside Press LLC

MMX

www.wildsidebooks.com

FIRST EDITION

CONTENTS

DEDICATED

TO THE INSPIRED SIGN-PAINTERS WHO LABEL
THE EXITS OFF INTERSTATE HIGHWAYS

THEY ARE THE PROGENITORS OF
LIVINGSTON FROST

PROLOGUE

I had an old friend who periodically took all the left-overs in her refrigerator and popped them into a pot to simmer. This usually became a rich and tasty soup, which her family ate enthusiastically—she called it her "make-'em-eat-it" soup.

This volume is my literary equivalent.

In 1999 my world as I knew it came to an end. Joe, my husband of forty-one years, died after a long illness. The next month I had a serious car wreck, which shattered my left foot and ankle and compressed my t-5 vertebra by fifty percent.

At the time I'd begun several novels, including the third Washington Shipp mystery, only a couple of which I was able to complete. Thereafter, my creativity seemed to be lost, and I have written very little since, though I kept on critiquing the work of new writers. So here are a few "orphans," which I would have loved to complete in fuller form, but couldn't—and can't. I have provided summarized endings to help complete the narratives.

I hope you enjoy them just the same.

—Ardath Mayhar
Chireno, Texas
November, 2009

BORN REBEL

(1825)

This is based on my own family history—my great-great-great grandmother left on her wedding day to come to Texas with her own choice of a husband. I can only guess what her would-be husband's (back in South Carolina) reaction might have been, much less her own family's. The couple did get across the Sabine River and had two children, one of whom was my great-great grandfather, David Cannon.

BORN REBEL

CHAPTER ONE

JUDITH MCCARRAN

Judith pushed a strand of hair out of her eyes with a sweaty sleeve and straightened her back. Leaning on her hoe, she stared along the corn row toward her nearest sister. Beyond Susan was her mother, and on other rows of the cornfield were the rest of her siblings, except for Lily, who lay in a horse collar at the end of the row, teething on a bit of licorice root, and her two married sisters.

"Get busy, there," her father growled behind her. "No time for lollygagging. We've got to get this corn thinned so we can go ahead with your wedding. You put your back into it, girl!"

Biting her lip, the young woman bent to her work again, battling her innate need to admit she hated her father. The preacher said you had to honor your father and your mother, but she had a hard time doing either. Mama was beaten to her knees, all the fight long ago knocked out of her. Pa was right up there beside God, a pair of unforgiving son-of-a-bitch if ever there was one.

Chopping the pale green shoots amid a fine haze of dust, Judith thought about that wedding. Her wedding, indeed! She had about as much to say about it as little Lily did. Pa wanted his family's hardscrabble acres hooked up with the adjoining Medlar property's rich river bottom stretches, and if it took marrying his third daughter to old man Oscar, that was fine. He didn't have to sleep with the filthy old devil or look after his two mean-spirited sons.

Judith paused again, wondering if God was going to strike her with lightning for thinking such blasphemy, but he didn't. Encouraged by the lack of celestial fireworks, she moved forward, both hoe and head busy.

Her sister Dena had two children after three years of marriage. Angela had one and expected another at any moment. Judith had no intention of bearing fourteen children, as her mother had.

Old Oscar had a wicked gleam in his eye when he looked at her, though so far she'd managed to avoid being alone with him. What would happen when she was shoved into his hands was something she hated to think about. She had even thought about killing herself to avoid being married to him, but she was too young and bright to carry it through.

She'd helped deliver Lily and Carrie and Stella and little Jonah, who'd died soon after being born. She knew too much about childbirth to have any great ambition to undertake it for herself unless it was for somebody she really loved and wanted to have a child by. Her heart felt heavy as she reached the end of the row.

Deep shadows of the mountain to the west already covered the field. Pa yelled, "Quitting time!" and headed toward the house. Once there, he'd wash up and sit on the stoop while the womenfolk added women's work to a full day of man's work, kindling the cookfire, frying cornbread and chicken. Once he and George and Thomas and DeLancy ate their fill, the women would eat a bit of whatever was left, wash up everything, and put the dirty clothing to soak for tomorrow's wash.

She wished now she'd married David McCarran when he asked. She'd had no desire to be wed to anybody, but

David was a far sight better than Oscar Medlar. He was kind, and she'd known him since they were in diapers. Better somebody you liked, she realized now that it was too late, than somebody you hated the sight of.

But David had taken her at her word, and Pa had forbidden him to come courting anyway. She saw him only at Meeting or when his own Pa sent him over to the DuBay farm on some errand. She wished he'd come to the wedding. At least there would be one sympathetic face in the bunch.

She knew he wouldn't, however. He had too much pride, and maybe he'd been hurt more than she thought when she said no. He'd hardly looked at her, the few times they saw each other since.

Supper over, the dishes washed, the table and floor scrubbed, the weary women went to the spring to bathe in the big wooden tub of water that had been warming in the sun all day. Judith helped her shorter sisters into and out of the spring to rinse off. When her own turn came she was almost too tired to move, but the sweat and dust of the day were pure misery.

The water felt good to her sunburned skin, and she took a quick dip in the creek, mother naked, after the others went back to the house. With reluctance, she donned her shift and went up to the hot little attic room she shared with Susan, Carrie, and Stella.

She could hear Lily's plaintive wails as she neared the stoop, and she hurried in with a bit of fresh root for the baby to suck as she went to sleep. Suddenly she hated everyone here, from the teething infant to her father, now reading the Bible aloud in his sonorous voice.

Judith realized suddenly that she hated the Bible, too. Now she really did expect to be struck down in her iniquity, but no blast came, not even a rumble of thunder. For the first time in her seventeen years, Judith DuBay wondered if there was any God at all; or was he something used by men to keep their women afraid and biddable?

Feeling incredibly sinful, she slipped past the door and climbed the porch post to cross the narrow roof and enter her bedroom through the window. She'd used that route in and out of the house since she was a little tad. Sometimes she'd gone out with David to follow, very stealthily, the men's possum hunts or to listen to the hounds belling through the woods after a coon.

She opened the shutters as wide as they'd go, letting the night breeze through the unglazed window. They were lucky to have a window at all; others sweated out their nights, she knew, in windowless boxes of rooms. At least Pa let Ma persuade him to cut openings into all the rooms.

If he'd known how much more comfortable it made his daughters, doubtless he'd have refused. He claimed suffering was a woman's lot in life, and nothing that eased it was acceptable to God or Man. The curse of Eve was on all women, he claimed, and the more they did penance, the better it was for their souls.

He and almost every other male she knew believed the same thing and seemed set on doing his part to make that suffering acute. And the day after tomorrow she'd belong, body and soul, to Oscar Medlar, whose reputation regarding treatment of his slaves was terrible and whose mouth had a cruel twist. The thought made her sick.

If she had a horse, she'd light out over the mountains toward the west. People she knew told of kin who had gone to Kentucky or Mississipp' or even to Texas. By now there ought to be fair-sized communities in those wild parts. Surely she could get on as a farm worker or such, if she only managed to escape.

But she knew better. Even there she'd be considered only female flesh, to be used and disregarded like her mother and most of the women she knew. Her father's horse and his mules were better regarded than she and her mother and sisters, and nobody ever pretended anything different.

David's mother was the only woman she had ever known who held her head high and spoke her mind. Her husband listened to her, too, as did others when there was a matter of importance that needed clear thinking. Elizabeth McCarran did not put up with any nonsense, even from the preacher.

It would have been wonderful if Caroline DuBay had possessed her spunk and intelligence. Maybe, if she had, Pa wouldn't have been so highhanded with other people's lives.

* * * * * * *

Despite Judith's dread, the day of the wedding arrived. Her white cotton dress was starched, ironed stiff with hours of backbreaking labor with flatirons, and hung from a hook in the wardrobe chest. Guests had already arrived, her aunts' families coming on a two-day journey to see her married. The house was full of small cousins.

Judith was up before dawn, busy with last minute cooking, packing up her few items of clothing, trying her best not to think of what would come after today. When Susan went down to the spring after water, just after sunrise, Judith was already tired and out of sorts.

She was glad when her mother motioned for her to go to her bedroom and begin getting ready. From now on, she must be out of sight of arriving guests and the bridegroom, for tradition was respected among their family.

She was leaning on the windowsill when she saw Susan run across the back yard, trying not to slosh water out of the wooden bucket. Strange—Susan seldom got into a hurry. When her sister's voice called at the door, after a few minutes, Judith wondered what might be afoot.

"Jude...Jude, go down to the spring and say goodbye to David. He's got..."—the girl paused to catch her breath—

"...he's got his slaves Joseph and Cassie with him, and horses, and they're going to Texas. He wants to see you before they take off."

There was an almost audible thump beneath Judith's breastbone. Was this the chance she had been praying for (yes, even though she now had grave doubts as to the existence of any god except Pa)? Had some miracle sent her the opportunity to escape her dreadful destiny?

Without pausing to think, she caught up the packed carpetbag and tossed it out of the window. She put on a pair of breeches George had outgrown, which she kept for working in the fields, took her shawl out of the wardrobe chest, and dragged her boots out from under the trundle bed where Carrie slept.

Then she climbed out that old familiar window, down the porch on the side screened by honeysuckle vines, and sped away toward the spring. Everyone, she knew quite well, was in the front parlor, making false faces and falser conversation, and not a single voice rose to call her back.

The path was crooked, overarched by huge hardwoods and edged with fern and stickery vines, but her stout boots crashed over any obstruction. David heard her coming, she knew, for he was standing at the end of the path, waiting for her, his ruddy face alight with sudden hope.

"David, you still want to marry me?" she panted, as she skidded to a stop. "If you do, let's hurry and leave, because there's going to be a ring-tailed twister of a fuss in just a few minutes, when Ma and the girls come to help me dress for the wedding and I'm not there."

He caught her in a mighty hug. Then he led the way across the foot log and boosted her onto Old Jess, his sorrel mare. Joseph and his wife were grinning, their teeth and the whites of their eyes shining in the shadows of the forest, as she turned to grin back.

Then they were moving single file through the thickly growing trees, following a game trail leading west. There lay more mountains, swamps, Indians, criminals of all stripes, rivers that drowned the unwary, and all sorts of unforeseen dangers. Judith felt ready to confront any or all of them. Compared to the prospect of being the wife of Oscar Medlar, facing perils in the wilderness seemed eminently preferable.

She turned in the saddle and smiled at David, who rode just behind her on Blue Roan. "How did you know I'd come?" she asked. "Or did you just hope?"

"I've been knowing you since you were knee high to a duck," he said. "I been thinking about you and old Oscar, and I could just about read your mind, even so far away. You'd never marry that old bastard if you had any choice in the matter. So I gave you a choice, that's all."

Judith sighed. Having someone who knew you so well, who cared enough to give you a chance, was a lovely thing to think about, now she'd had a taste of what the alternative might have been. David was clean as new split wood, kind as a mother cat, and she knew he respected her, whether or not she might be female. His family had far different ideas on that matter.

The thought reminded her. "Where can we get married?" she asked him, bending to keep her thick coil of auburn hair from catching on a low-sweeping branch. "I've never been over this way and I don't even know what towns are there."

David grunted. "I know just the place. Pa's Cousin Martin is the preacher at the Pine Knot Settlement half a day's ride beyond the river. Our Newberry kinfolk settled there a piece back, and I know Cousin Martin will tie the knot for us without any fuss or bother."

It was still early, and sunlight shafted down through the thick layers of branches and leaves. Squirrels chattered and scampered along the thick limbs, paying no heed to the riders far below them. The day felt fresh and clean and new, and she realized her own life did, as well.

Judith experienced a sense of freedom unlike any she had ever known in all her constricted life. She felt as if she could shinny up one of the big oaks or maples and play tag with the squirrels, if she wanted to. Many was the time her Ma had scolded her, when she was little, for just such antics. She had a feeling David would only laugh if she climbed a tree, instead of going pale with shock and dismay as her own kin did.

When they came to the river, the water was high, but all the horses were strong swimmers; their riders came out on the other side pretty well damped down but without mishap. They stopped to build a fire and dry off, and Judith took the opportunity to change George's breeches for her own gray cotton skirt. It seemed fit, somehow, to get married looking more like a girl than a boy.

Yet the sun went down long before they reached the Settlement, and they stopped again, this time for the night. Amid the hoots of owls, the chirring of crickets, the mournful calls of a whippoorwill, and occasional screams of a distant painter, she helped Cassie cook bacon and skillet bread.

She had no qualm about settling herself beside David for the night. He was her friend, and she knew he would never push her for anything she wasn't yet ready to give. Her back was warm where it touched his blanketed shape, and that was a comfort.

Joseph was on the first watch, his figure dark against the faint glow of the covered coals. Cassie, pregnant and uncomfortable, whimpered in her sleep from time to time.

But Judith, free and happy in her escape from a miserable marriage, slept at once. She never stirred until David shook her gently, when dawn was only a thin line in the eastern sky and the birds of morning were beginning their sleepy trills.

"Wake up, Lady," he whispered. "Today's our wedding day."

And this time the words did not toll like funeral bells in her heart.

* * * * * *

The Settlement was tucked into a narrow valley that ran up beside a river flowing down the mountains. Here and there were fields of corn or cotton or tobacco, set amid patches of woodland. Houses were few but stoutly built of logs, and those early-birds working among the rows straightened their backs and hailed the travelers in a friendly manner.

Cousin Martin was one of them. His cornfield was beside his two-room house, and when David recognized him, knee deep in young corn, he yelled, "Come out of the field, Cousin, and meet my intended. We want to get married—you still a preacher?"

The tall, thick shape straightened, pushed back his wide hat, and spat between his teeth before he began moving toward the road. "That sounds like young David. What you doin' so far from home, boy?"

David had dismounted, now, and Joseph was helping Judith down from Jess. Together they went to meet the big fellow, and he put his hands on his hips and grinned at them. "You runnin' away together?" he asked. "I hate to help young'uns spite their families." But he didn't sound as if he meant a word of it.

Mittie, Martin's wife, had come out of the house, wiping her hands on her apron. Now she called to the group in the road, "You all come in here out of the sun and tell me what in tunket is going on. We don't get any excitement here from year's end to year's end, so if any is happening, I want to be in the big middle of it."

They climbed up the split log steps and settled onto hickory splint chairs on the wide porch. Everybody seemed to be talking at once, but before they were done,

Martin and Mittie understood the situation and agreed to hold the wedding, then and there.

"Seems a shame not to have more to do over it, but I guess you do what you can with what you have," Mittie mourned. "I'd purely like to have a dance and a shivaree for you two, but I reckon if Oscar Medlar may be coming after you, you'd better get hitched and light out."

Her husband nodded. "That man has a mean streak that we hear about, even way over here. He killed one of his slaves for skinnin' up one of the riding horses, they tell me, just up and whacked him to death with his walking stick. I wouldn't let a dog of mine live with him, much less one of my daughters. Your Pa must not...." He caught himself before he insulted Judith's family.

"My Pa tried to sell me for some land," she said, her tone dry. "David has saved my life, I suspect. Preacher Martin. Now let's get this done so we can light out for Texas."

* * * * * * *

Formally witnessed by Mittie, her grown daughter Letitia, and their neighbor Josh Tate, Judith's wedding took place in the front yard of the small house, surrounded by flowering jasmine and growing herbs. Joseph and Callie watched, too, and Judith wondered if they thought this sort of pairing was any stranger than their own informal but binding rituals.

Somehow, jumping over a broomstick had a more daring ring to it...but she shook aside the thought and answered the preacher's question with a resounding, "Yes!"

Once the vows were made, Martin painstakingly wrote out their wedding lines in find copperplate script, with the date, the place, the minister, and the witnesses all properly listed. He copied it for his own records and when that was done, the newly wedded pair left, amid good wishes and a few tears.

Mittie had been inconsolable. "The least we can do is cook up a wedding meal," she protested, but Martin was as firm as David.

"Medlar won't stand around and wait. As soon as he knew Judith was gone, I know he must've started figurin' a way to follow her and stop them. I can't think of anythin' worse than havin' her carried back to Newberry, leavin' David dead behind her, to suffer the vengeance of that evil man. Let 'em go, Mittie. We'll pray for 'em. That'll do a lot more good, in the long run."

Judith agreed. Her blood chilled in her veins at the thought of what might happen if Medlar or one of his henchmen overtook them now.

BORN REBEL

CHAPTER TWO

JONAS BLUTH

When Oscar Medlar's slave Sully rode up to his shack-ledy porch, Jonas was dozing in the shade, his feet propped against the front wall of his shanty, his head drooping over the edge of the uneven boards. After a drunk, he could sleep on a rock with a snake, he'd decided long ago.

But Sully wouldn't go away, even when Jonas shied a loose board at him. "Marse Oscar, he wants to see you right now, Suh," the man said. "Said he's got a job for you that's got to be did right off, if it's did a'tall."

Jonas opened one eye, hoping his bleary glare would frighten Sully into the next county, but Sully had long experience dealing with white men, and he didn't budge. Knowing Oscar's mean temper, Jonas couldn't much blame him.

He sighed and heaved himself into a sitting position. "What in tarnation does the old man want now?" he grumbled, scratching under his armpit. "He's got more money, more land, and more gall than anybody I know. What might he need that he ain't already got?"

"A wife." Sully grinned, his teeth shining in his ebony face. "Miz Judith, she up and run away wid de McCarrans' youngest boy. Right there on her weddin' day. I 'spect Marse Oscar wants somebody to go atter 'em and bring her back. Course, I don't know for certain, but seems as if it's in his mind."

Jonas let out a snort of laughter. He'd wondered if that high-headed DuBay woman would stand for being traded off to old Oscar for the tract of land next to her pa, and it seemed he was right. He'd caught her in the woods one day picking up hickory nuts. When he tried to kiss her, she'd knocked him flat with her snake stick, and run so fast he never came in sight of her till she stopped at her own porch.

Oscar Medlar ought to be glad she was gone. If he'd made her mad, she might've done even worse to him.

He spat into the bushes that had grown up along his porch and rose slowly, pulling up his pants to a decent level. "Be right with you," he said to Sully. "You ride on toward home, and I'll come behind, soon as I ketch old Mossback."

"You go an' do what you needs to do," the slave replied. "I'll get yo' horse for you. He still kep' in the lot out back?"

Jonas nodded and turned to get his shirt and hat. It'd be nice to have a slave to do your work, he thought. But then you'd have to feed the bastard, and sometimes it was as much as he could do to feed himself. Last good pay he'd had was when that new slave of the De Peysters ran off and he tracked him down. Maybe Oscar would pay well for getting his runaway bride back.

Jonas grinned as he put on his filthy shirt and his sweaty hat. The sooner he got there, the sooner he'd know.

* * * * * * *

Sully had Mossback saddled and ready when he went outside, though the gelding was snorting and stamping with irritation. When Jonas got drunk, the horse always had a couple of days of idleness, and he evidently didn't like this change in his habits.

"Giddap!" Jonas kicked him in the ribs and they moved at an easy pace toward the Medlar farm. It would be twilight before they arrived, so he could look forward to a good supper and a soft bed for the night.

He found he was wrong. Medlar was waiting on his veranda, his frog mouth turned down at the corners and his eyes squinted with fury. "You've got to catch those two," he roared as soon as the riders came into view.

"Bluth, you go round to the kitchen. Mary's got you a pack of provisions and a couple of blankets. You got to ride tonight. I know they'll move fast. That McCarran bastard's got more sense than most, even if he is a thief. You've got to bring that woman back to me. I'll make her crawl before I'm done.

"Nobody leaves Oscar Medlar at the altar, with the whole neighborhood standing around snickering and making jokes. I'll make her regret the day she got on that horse and rode away from me, and her Pa won't raise a hand to save her.

"He's disowned her, though that woman he married told me to my face she was glad her daughter was gone. I wouldn't have thought she had the nerve, and I'll bet Rupert beat her good once everybody left."

Jonas stared into the narrow black eyes. "Better I get going than stand here talkin'," he said. "You know which way they planned to go?"

"That girl Susan said McCarran told her he was headed to Texas. That's a long way, with no law to speak of between here and there and no regular road to give you any idea of how they intend to head out. They've prob'ly crossed the river by now.

"If you don't catch 'em before they get married, you kill David and the slaves and bring Judith back to me. Or kill her, if that's the only way, but scalp her for proof. That way anybody that takes notice'll think the Injuns killed 'em."

Jonas's grin was genuine, now. "What're you goin' to pay for this hard and dangerous job?" he asked. "I don't put my neck in a noose for anybody, without they make it worth my while."

"I got gold to pay with. Lots of it, and here's the first half in this sack. I'll make you a gift of my Halbach pistol when you get back. Here's enough coin to travel with, and the rest'll be waitin' for you."

Jonas's heart warmed. "The pistol with the eagle on the butt cap?" he asked, trying to mask the enthusiasm in his voice.

"The very same. What do you say?" Medlar's wicked eyes squinted, and his mouth tried to look friendly but failed.

"I'm gone already." Jonas suited his actions to his words, moving Mossback around to the kitchen of the sprawling house. There Mary, the cook, handed up a heavy pack, which he arranged behind his saddle.

When he rode away along the dusty road in the moonlight, he took a quick glance back. Medlar wasn't watching. Must be satisfied that his job would be done right, Jonas thought with satisfaction. Which it would be.

Jonas Bluth had never failed to take his man or woman. This time would be no different.

He kicked Mossback into a lope and headed for the river. That was the first holdup, and he might just catch them there if they'd had some mishap along the way. If not, there were a lot of miles betwixt here and Texas, Even if he didn't cut their trail for a while, he'd come up with his prey someplace along the way.

The thought of scalping Judith DuBay appealed to him more and more. Oscar'd never know whether it was necessary or not, and if he killed the rest first, he could tend to her at his leisure, leaving the scalping until last. Teach her to be so high and mighty!

BORN REBEL

CHAPTER THREE

LUCY MCCARRAN DEWITT

The McCarran porch was a billow of skirts, as the six quilters sat about the frame, finishing off the quilt in progress. As the busy hands stitched, the tongues were even busier discussing David and Judith, who had eloped to Texas just a week before. The fact that three of the quilters were David's two sisters and his mother didn't spare him.

It was bad enough having your youngest brother take off for God-knows-where, Lucy decided, but for him to leave behind the kind of hornet's nest he did was unforgivable. She'd been grateful when that high-headed Judith refused his proposal...the McCarrans were gentlefolk, not like those DuBay riffraff, too poor even to own slaves to do their field work.

She looked down at the soft hands holding her needle, proud that they had never pulled a weed or touched a hoe. This allowed her to avoid Mama's eye, of course, and to keep from showing her shame at her brother's irresponsibility. Just like him to run off and leave her to face the gossip.

That hussy Judith occupied her thoughts, too. The idea of running away from a bridegroom with the land and wealth Oscar Medlar possessed in order to go with a man she wasn't married to (and might not ever be, as far as

Lucy could tell) was abhorrent. The buzz of voices around her never let that subject rest for long, and Lucy felt hot and uncomfortable, though she managed to hide it.

Husband Robert had declared their position in the matter as soon as they arrived and found what had happened. "We shall simply ignore the entire situation," he told his wife. "Even if your own mother wants to speak of it, you will refuse, Lucinda. I forbid you to discuss it or to acknowledge the existence of that shameless pair."

That suited Lucy to a T. She had no desire to face the storm of criticism now leveled at her brother and potential sister-in-law. Only with her sister Anne, who had also arrived to take part in this annual family gathering, would she have liked to speak of the matter.

She would find an opportunity, she felt certain. What Robert didn't know he could not object to. She had kept other secrets from him in the four years of their marriage.

She had a suspicion he had not been entirely candid with her as well, though that was, of course, a man's prerogative. A woman had to be content with what a husband granted to her, and Lucy had never understood how her mother could be so resistant to that idea.

Even now, Elizabeth was saying, in her quiet drawl, "If I'd been Judith, I'd have run away, too. Oscar Medlar is a libertine. I've delivered more than one of his get to unmarried women around here, not all of 'em black."

How could she! Lucy felt herself blushing to her very toes. Mama was simply not a part of the world Lucy approved or understood. She thought of the jar of wild carrot seed Elizabeth had set into her hands as she and Robert drove away on their wedding day.

"Don't have children you don't want," her mother had told her. "Take a spoonful in water every morning, until you're ready to conceive. No use being pregnant all the time like poor Caroline DuBay."

The very idea had shocked Lucy profoundly. You had

babies when God sent them, Preacher Bogard taught his flock. Anything else was unthinkable.

She'd dropped the jar quietly into a ditch and never thought about it again, except when they came back home for a visit and saw the tangle of lacy white blossoms there in the ditch where the jar had landed. Now that she was pregnant for the third time, with the baby only four months old, Lucy had begun to wonder if she hadn't been a mite hasty.

Anne's voice brought her out of her reverie. "I think David may do well in Texas," she was saying. "My Faron knows a family who went in that direction a year past, and there's been word from them just recently. They squatted on land they say will sprout seeds so fast they'll hit you in the face, if you don't back up fast enough.

"The letter that came by way of a wagoneer was full of praise for the place. Said the Spanish give them no trouble, so far, being busy with a rebellion on their home ground, and the Indians haven't made any ruckus to speak of."

How could she? Lucy suddenly felt a surge of nausea. Morning sickness was still plaguing her, and she excused herself to go to the side yard and throw up into the cape jasmine bush. It wasn't enough to be sick and miserable, to have to nurse a baby with another one tugging on her coat tail, but she had to be faced with this sickening disgrace. It was just too bad.

She felt a cool hand come over her shoulder to touch her cheek. "So you're hatching again," said Anne's calm voice. "I thought that might be the problem. It's almighty hot, and that always makes it worse. I'm glad I haven't decided to stop taking the seeds yet."

Lucy, stunned, turned to face her sister. "You mean you took them? After what the preacher said? It's next door to a sin, I'd say." She wiped her face on her handkerchief and gulped a deep breath to quiet her stomach.

"How do you think Mama got away with just having

four, instead of the scads of children all the other women hereabout have?" Anne asked. "She did the same. It's no man's place to tell me how many children to have, if I can manage to have just what I want and no more."

Lucy felt she was the only one in the entire clan who cared a jot what either Man or God might think of her behavior. But she said nothing. Arguing with a McCarran was like butting a stump. You got a headache from it, and the stump never changed its position a bit.

As she returned to the porch and her interrupted patch of quilting, Lucy was filled with resentment. Lacking a more accessible object, she focused all of it on Judith Du-Bay. Even if David married her—and why should he if he could have her without marriage? She would never accept the woman as a sister, no matter what happened.

She hoped she'd never see or hear of her again. And if she ever had a chance to give back a bit of the pain this disgrace had caused her, Lucy was sure she'd not hesitate a minute.

BORN REBEL

CHAPTER FOUR

DAVID MCCARRAN

Grandsir McCarran had settled in South Carolina before the War for Independence, when David's father was a boy. Hard work, sensible wives, and industrious ways had resulted in the family's present prosperity. When Fleming McCarran married Elizabeth MacArdle, he had possessed hundreds of acres, dozens of slaves, and a solid house that had already stood for almost a half century.

Having the good sense to consult with his wife before making changes, Fleming had found his wealth growing and his problems diminishing. No longer was there a problem getting his slaves to work willingly; the treatment Elizabeth insisted upon for them made them healthy and happy, and he learned that was all it took to have good workers.

His sons George and David learned the lesson well, and by the time Fleming died the farm was running smoothly. It had never been David's intention to work with his brother, knowing George intended to use him as an overseer while depriving him of any share in the profits or the land, even those acres their mother had brought to the marriage.

Elizabeth would never have allowed this to happen, if women had possessed any right in their own possessions, but under the law they were property. Father might have listened to her, but early in his life he had decided primogeniture to be the only way to keep the great stretches of the combined properties together. George inherited, and David resolved to leave as soon as he could.

His mother understood fully. It had been she who made sure he would have his slave Joseph and his mulatto wife, as well as enough gold to make certain he could buy what he needed on the journey to Texas and to pay for land, if necessary, once he got there. Who knew if the news about grants from Spain were true? It was best to be prepared for whatever came.

George would have objected, if he dared, but Elizabeth had secured to herself a store of gold, using methods even David never managed to guess. And now he was on his way, with extra mounts, supplies for a very long journey, and his two valued slaves.

He had never really dared to hope that Judith would change her earlier decision, far less that she would accompany him as his wife. The hard trail he had faced was suddenly easier. His life, which had seemed likely to be both lonely and gloomy, suddenly brightened.

She had come down the shadowy path, answering his call, her thick coil of auburn hair glinting in occasional shafts of sunlight, her steady gray eyes raised to his in inquiry.

Would he marry her and take her with him? What a question! Only after they were well on their way, after their brief wedding, did David begin to worry about how to approach his new wife. She was so much like his mother that he never considered forcing himself upon her, no matter how much he might want her. As it turned out, this was not a problem.

He had never managed to outguess his mother, and his wife was going to be no different. With her usual directness, Judith turned to him as they camped for the night. "I am now your wife, David, and I intend to do what is right; find us a private place, for I am embarrassed to sleep with you, so near to your people."

Only she could possibly have come out with it in such a straightforward way, without blushing or beating about the bushes. He almost laughed, though he knew that would have been fatal.

Instead, he nodded gravely. "I will go and look for someplace that is private, yet is not so far away that Joseph cannot keep watch for any danger in the night."

He located a leafy spot, sheltered by the leaning trunk of a huge oak. And there, though there were surprises for them both, he consummated their marriage, feeling with some dismay that Judith's obvious pain and his own difficulty were somehow his fault.

Yet he comforted her, and when he again made love to her the pain was less, leaving him with hope that things would be better later. Her hard work in the fields must have affected her body more than one would think, he decided.

After that their days were so long, so difficult, and so filled with effort that neither of them had the energy for anything except sleep. They climbed steep, wooded mountains, coming out atop bare slopes of stone from which they could see for miles across river bottoms and endless forest.

As they traveled, David occupied his thoughts with plans for the future. He talked quietly with Judith in the night, sharing with her his discoveries among those who had received word from kin already in Texas.

"There are very few Anglos, as they call us, in the place to which we are headed," he told her. "The last word the Quentins had was that the local Indians are friendly, and the white community is growing slowly, as others come into the country.

"The Mexican government seems not to object to having this empty country colonized. Not many of their own people want to leave Mexico City to live in such a primitive spot. It may be that we can gain official title to the land we choose, without having to use any of Mama's gold."

He knew Judith too well to doubt that the prospect of rich land, free for the working, appealed to her as much as to him. She was the child of generations of farmers, and he had always known she loved even the hard field work she had done all her life. Her eyes brightened in the firelight as he talked, and he could see his own dreams for the future reflected there.

They went on in hope, struggling through swamps, over mountains, along rivers that held no ferry or bridge or even farm for many miles. They were moving along such a stream, bitten by gnats and mosquitoes, their feet thick with mud and their horses snorting and snuffling, when an arrow thunked into a willow beside David's head.

He dropped instantly into the tangle of button willow, snakeweed, and thick grass, hearing his companions' movements as they followed suit. Someone, probably Judith, slapped a horse, which dashed away noisily along the game trail they had been following.

David hissed softly. In reply he heard a twitter that was Joseph's version of a willow wren, another hiss, which was Judith, and a flutter, which was Cassie's best effort at a whistle. So. All were safe, so far.

He silently loaded his musket, checked his knife in its sling at his side, and slipped on his belly along the ground, concealed by the thick growth along the stream. At that level the small animals made their own roads, and he found runways along which he could slither without making much sound.

It was hot down there, and sweat stung his eyes and trickled around his rib cage as he crawled, but he had noted the angle of the arrow in the willow. Its owner would be somewhere in this direction, and if he could, he was going to locate and kill him. David had no intention of losing his family at this point in his life.

He had not thought Joseph would do anything except wait for him to act, but in a moment he heard, off to his right, a gurgle and a swish, as if some uncontrolled motion disturbed the brush. David paused, listening. Then, directly ahead, he heard another movement. Someone there had also heard the small sounds and was moving to investigate.

David waited, straining his ears to catch almost inaudible frictions of leaf upon leaf or twig under moccasin, until he had located his quarry. Then he rose, musket ready, and charged toward the area just ahead of the last detected sound.

The bronzed shape turned swiftly, bringing up his bow, but David's musket roared, black smoke filled the air, and the Indian went down. David dropped again at once, but there was no more disturbance in the wood along the little river.

Joseph came stooping along a path. "That's both on 'em, Sah," he said. "I got the other 'un over there in the bushes. Looks like Cherokee to me, Sah. They been movin' west, folks says. Likely we done found hunters for a bigger bunch, you think?"

It was more than likely, David thought. He had known families that had moved onto the lands of the Cherokee, back in the east, taking over their well tended fields, even their big houses, and seizing their slaves.

Though it was plain that God meant the white man to rule this new world, he wondered how he might feel if someone came out of nowhere and took what he had worked hard to produce. But it was a troubling thought, and he shook it away as the two of them returned to the river bank where the women waited.

"Stand!" came the challenge. Judith's voice. She knew

to load her weapon and keep watch until the outcome of the encounter was clear.

"Just us," he called softly. "We got them, Wife. Now we better go on as fast as we can, because they may have angry relatives coming along almost any minute."

Before they had gone far, they caught up with the horse that had been used to distract the attackers. He had stopped in a patch of tender grass and was not pleased when they led him forward.

They went fast, and before the sun had moved much across the sky they found a ford that was not too dangerous to try. The early rains had dwindled now, and the water was half down the steep banks. At one spot deer evidently came down to drink, wearing a slot in the sandy-red soil; down this cut they rode to a tiny beach leading into the mud-colored stream.

Jess snorted as she stepped into the water, dancing as if she were afraid, though David knew it to be an act she always performed, no matter who rode her. Behind Joseph and Cassie, riding Blue Roan, David shepherded his group across the stretch of water, watching sharply for floating debris. He'd known more than one person to drown, pushed under by a floating log or other unexpected flotsam on a river or creek.

Water moccasins were lively in the heat of summer, and he saw two swimming in the shallows, their wicked heads just above water, their long bodies flexing gently with the ripples.

"Watch out when you go ashore," he called to Judith. "There's a lot of snakes about. And don't dismount until you can see your footing clear and plain."

The way Jess picked her way up the farther bank, David knew she hadn't missed those mottled shapes. The mare went forward to a stretch of grass and only then would she consent to stop and rest. They all took pains to watch their footing as they moved about the small clearing, getting a bit of food and going into the bushes to relieve themselves.

Judith asked, as they got ready to move again, "Do you think crossing the river will keep those angry relatives from following us? We leave a mighty plain trail, whatever we do."

David had been thinking about that, but he knew the horses had to be rested or his people would all be afoot in this unforgiving country. "I think maybe those folks are out of their own country, just the way we are. Could be, they don't know their way around any better than we do. They don't know what enemies they might find this side of the river, and that should work for us." He chuckled wryly. "Then, of course, we don't know that either, do we?"

He checked the river from the shelter of the brush behind which they were hidden. No shadowy figure was visible beyond the tawny ripples of the stream, and nothing disturbed the water itself. Still, it would be foolish to follow the dim trail that had led them so far. It was time to strike off into the wilderness, using only the stars and the sun and their own native wits for guidance.

He did not mount, and the others followed his example. Moving through the heavy forest did not mean concealment by undergrowth. Here the trees were old, their branches interlocked overhead, shading the thick mulch of the forest floor, where no bushes and few vines seemed to grow.

This meant easy going for both horses and people, but a rider was more visible and more vulnerable than one afoot. A walker was always able to duck behind tree trunks or drop to the ground, but when you rode you were exposed to anyone who might be in hiding.

Only Cassie rode, for she was now growing too heavy and unbalanced to risk on the ground. David felt increasing uneasiness about her, and he knew Joseph shared his concern.

The young woman's face, usually tawny gold, was grayish, and her eyes seemed sunken and rimmed with bruises. She didn't look good at all; he'd watched over and doctored enough of the family's female slaves to understand more than most men about such things as childbearing.

He asked Judith about the situation, that night after they halted to camp. She nodded slowly, her gaze following Cassie as she moved carefully about the fire. "I think the baby's coming very soon. You can see it has dropped already, and she walks differently now from the way she did a month ago, when we started out.

"I haven't helped Mama with all those babies without learning things she thinks it's not proper for an unmarried girl to know. Now that I'm married, I suppose she'd think it was all right." She laughed, but there was an edge to her voice that told him she resented many things about her mother.

David understood. It had often seemed to him that Judith would have been a more suitable daughter for Elizabeth, while his sister Lucy would have suited the DuBays down to the ground. He said nothing of that, however. If Judith had been his sister, he would have set out for Texas alone.

* * * * * * *

The easy going under the big trees lasted for three days, after which they found themselves facing a complex of creeks that formed a swampy area too dangerous to try, either afoot or on horseback. Even while they moved along its boundaries, looking for a ridge along which they might travel, they saw more than one deer and even a wild pig dash into the lush green morass and sink out of sight. Their struggles and the sounds of anguish they made were all the warning David needed.

They camped beside the swamp at last, knowing they must go north again to pick up the dim track they had been following before crossing the river. That night, after the tiny cookfire was quenched, Joseph came to David and gestured for him to follow him into the darkness.

"What is it, Joseph?" he asked his old friend. "Is something wrong?"

They stood beside a tangle of willows, listening to the night for a moment before proceeding. Then Joseph said, "Marse David, I been feelin' somethin' behind us. Can't see nothin', can't hear nothin', but I know it's there. You know my Mama she could witch things up, when she was a mind to. I got the gif', she told me. I been usin' the juju bones. They tells me we got trouble comin' after us."

David would have laughed, if he had not had his own specific warnings from old Seline, all the time he was growing up. She'd told him not to go on the hunt that had resulted in a moccasin bite that took months to heal up. She'd predicted his father's death to the day and the hour. No, if Seline said Joseph had her gift, David wasn't one to doubt her.

"They tell you we have someone chasing after us?" he asked, wondering if it might be the Indians beyond the river or maybe Oscar Medlar. Or could it be someone Judith's people sent to bring her back? Rupert DuBay was a stubborn man, though he had no money with which to pay for such work.

"I see a big man, when I looks at the bones. He got a bushy beard, some white, some black, and he rides a big old horse with a white star on its face. I got a name in my mind, but it's from what I knows, not from the bones. You 'member that man Bluth that's the slave catcher?"

As soon as he spoke the name, David knew he was right. He had instincts of his own, and they all chimed in to agree with his slave's warning. He'd been taking pains to hide what he could of their trail long before they had met the two Cherokee hunters. Cousin Martin's warnings had not gone unheeded.

"I've been having a feeling, myself," he told Joseph. "But all we can do is go on and try our best not to get careless. If it's Bluth back there, he's smart and he's mean.

"He knows how people act when they're running away, so the best thing I can see is to go the most direct way, as if we hadn't a care in the world. Then if he catches us, we'll be ready for him, and he won't expect that."

The dim form before him nodded, a shadow of motion in the darkness. "I reckon you're right, Sah," Joseph said. "But I been worry 'bout Cassie. She don't feel a bit good, and the fu'ther we go, the worse she feels. You think the baby gone come soon? That's goin' to set us back a bit, if it do."

"We'll worry about that when it happens," David said. "We'll just head back north of the swamp till we find that wagon track, and then we'll go for Natchez and the Miss'sipp as fast as we can. If we stop, we stop, but we'll go on when it's possible.

"You just keep your knife to hand and I'll keep the rifle loaded, except for flint. Judith's got Pa's flintlock pistol, and she keeps it ready. Give Cassie the skinning knife. If one of us doesn't get that bastard, maybe another one will."

Even as he spoke, he felt a sense of unreality. Surely this was just superstition. There was no way to know about anything that was behind you, he argued with himself. Yet his spine had chilled and his neck prickled as they traveled, as if some distant ill-wisher were stalking him. Joseph's juju only confirmed his own suspicions.

No, from here on they would move as an army moved in enemy territory, weapons ready, wits alert. If someone, Bluth or another or even some totally unexpected adversary, moved against them, he might be completely surprised at their reaction.

BORN REBEL

CHAPTER FIVE

JUDITH MCCARRAN

If she had been lifted by a whirlwind and carried away into unknown territory, Judith could not have felt more disoriented. Though she had known for years that Pa intended to trade her for the land along the Medlar property line, somehow the reality of that marriage had never sunk in until the day of the wedding.

Even now she shuddered when she thought how close she had come to belonging to that cruel and arrogant man. She had felt hopeless, without any chance of reprieve. Then Susan brought the word that David waited at the spring, and suddenly she knew what to do.

Now she wondered why she had declined David's offer two years ago. Compared to Oscar Medlar, even the overworked field hands looked preferable, whatever their race. David was a real prize.

David was no saint, but he was now her husband and she had no regrets. She had gone into this marriage without any illusions. A farm girl knew all about life as soon as she was big enough to watch the cats and the cows and the horses at their birthing and begetting.

She had felt no need for such herself, but she knew she owed to her husband the thing men seemed to value above almost anything else. It had never occurred to her that it would hurt so badly or be so messy, but somehow David had soothed and eased her, without making her feel guilty. Perhaps, in time, she would come to value the exercise for itself.

The journey, however, was the main thing. When David told her about Joseph's juju bones and his own intuition that someone followed their trail, she was at first a bit skeptical. Then, thinking it over as they rode, she began to consider what might have been done by those they left behind them.

The next time they walked to rest the horses, she moved up close behind her husband. "David, what if Oscar Medlar sent somebody after us, the way your cousin thought he might? We've lived neighbors to him for years, and every time somebody out traded him or insulted him or just got on the wrong side of him, he managed someway to get even.

"Pa thought for years he had Old Man Scullers drowned because of that famous horse trade people still snicker about. Think about it. What could anybody do that would hurt his pride worse than what I've done?" She saw David nod, as he thought it over.

"Oscar's a mean devil; even my Pa always said that," he admitted, "not to mention Cousin Martin. He'd send somebody to catch us, if he could, and I wouldn't trust him not to give him orders to kill us all. So we better be almighty cautious, all the way."

He turned to look at her slantways. "I think you're right. I've been wondering how your Pa could manage to pay anybody to chase us, and I know he couldn't. Oscar could do it without turning a hair."

After that they kept closer watch at night, and though David had intended to take as direct a route as possible, now they took the main trail heading west. They found even that to be less than a good, clear track through the forest.

Besides that worry, there was Cassie, growing more and more uncomfortable as the days passed, until at last she began to moan as she rode, not loudly but as if the groans were forced out of her. When they stopped, early because of the clouds building in the southeast, the girl's tawny gold skin was ashy pale, and her labor had obviously begun.

To make it worse, the wind began to gust, promising a storm to come. Judith helped David and Joseph haul a tarpaulin into place, tying it down to saplings in a tiny clearing. They put Cassie under its shelter and turned to the horses, getting the packs under cover and tethering the mounts to convenient trees.

Lightning began lancing down the sky, with cracks of thunder getting nearer and nearer until one bolt struck a tall pine beyond the clearing. Judith heard a shrill whinny and the pound of hooves.

"One of the horses broke loose," she yelled above the snapping of the tarp and the whine of wind.

Joseph bolted out of the shelter after the animal, while Judith crawled to Cassie's side and felt for her hand in the dim light. The girl's skin was damp with sweat, and her face was twisted with pain.

"Something isn't right here," Judith called to David.

He moved in the dimness, and kindled his lantern to light the task ahead. "We need to see what we're doing," he said, kneeling on the other side of the girl. "I've been thinking she doesn't look good at all. Now that things are ready to happen, I hope luck's with us."

"Jody!" Cassie screamed suddenly, her voice blending with a peal of thunder.

"He'll be back. You just hang on and push, and we'll get this young one into the world without him." Judith's voice was firm, though she felt some sympathy for this very young woman, having her first child in a storm without her husband beside her.

The tarpaulin flapped like a captured eagle, trying to break free of its tethers. Even the chimney of the lantern didn't entirely shield its flame from the gusting wind, and sometimes spatters of rain swept under the shelter to sizzle on the hot glass. But in the yellow glow of its light, Judith found herself oblivious to the weather.

This was a breech birth, and Judith remembered all too clearly the small brother she had helped usher into the world, all bent and squashed after coming feet first. He had died before he breathed, and she had been young enough then, tenderhearted enough, to cry for him. Afterward, of course, she considered him lucky to escape the hard hands of his Pa and the unending labor of the farm from which he would receive no benefit other than the food he ate.

David looked up at her, a deep crease between his brows showing his worry. "Judith, your hands are smaller than mine. I helped Sudie's girl Jinks last spring with a breech. The secret lies in getting your hands right inside with it and turning it so the face isn't pushed so tight against the wall of the canal that it smothers.

"You can hold the legs as they come out, so the back doesn't kink and the neck doesn't break. I wouldn't ask you to do this, if my hands weren't so damn huge. Cassie's built smaller than Jinks is."

She frowned with concentration as she set her hands as he directed, working her fingers inside the hot, pulsing birth canal. Sure enough, once she had them in place she found she could put her fingers on either side of the tiny nose, keeping it free of the wall, while the infant slid down, held by her wrists and arms, to slip free at last.

It was a girl, limp and blue at first, but David caught her into those big hands and smacked her bottom. With a sort of gurgling whoop, the lungs expanded, pushed out the debris of birth, and the baby began to cry. It was only a small mew of sound, but Judith felt a huge smile growing within her.

Judith took the cotton cloth she had ready and wiped the infant clean, oiling her with tallow from their cooking supply. When she looked at David, her smile was reflected on his face.

They had done it! Under the most difficult of circumstances, they had saved both mother and baby. Now David cleaned his hands and bent to take up his musket. "Better go and help Joseph," he said. "We can't risk losing him in all this dark and wind."

Sitting in the flimsy shelter, in darkness now they had quenched the lantern, Judith waited beside the sleeping woman and her baby. The whip of the wind, the snap of the canvas. the swish of surrounding branches concealed any other noise, though she strained her ears, trying to hear any sound of the returning men.

At last she pushed together a heap of debris, twigs and leaves, and a few chunks of rotted wood, and kindled a small blaze, using flint and steel to start the fire. The darkness was too total, the noise too great to endure. By that small light she watched flickers of branches and leaves whipping in the wind, dead leaves skittering past, hints of motion she could not identify.

And then she was looking directly into the amber eyes of a panther, which appeared as if by magic and stood with its head just beneath the shelter. Ignoring her, it stared at the mother and child, and Judith recalled with horror the tales she had heard about the creatures' attraction to the infants of humankind.

She had been sitting with her flintlock pistol in her lap, primed and ready, for in this wild place there was no safety. Now she raised it stealthily, a fraction of an inch at a time, as the panther skirted the tiny fire as if disdaining it and moved into the rude tent.

The flash and roar of the firearm blinded and deafened her, and she scrabbled for her knife. If she hadn't killed it, the thing would have to be dealt with somehow, and the blade was all there was left. She had a fleeting sadness; David and Joseph would return to find themselves widowers, she was almost sure.

Then she could see through the cloud of black smoke that the wind was clearing away. The beast lay stretched across the skimpy floor, its head almost upon Cassie's pallet. The girl was awake, her eyes wide and terrified, her face even paler than before, as she hugged the baby to her and scrunched as far back as possible from the dead animal.

"It's dead, Cassie," Judith said, finding that her voice was barely a whisper. "I shot it. You can stretch out. We don't want to start that bad bleeding again." This time she managed to sound a bit more normal, and she helped the girl to ease her position and returned the infant to the pallet beside her.

"I'll see if I can drag him out of here. He smells like all the tomcats in tarnation, all rolled into one." But the long, tawny body was incredibly heavy in death, and strain as she might, she could move the beast only a short distance. At least he was out of the shelter, where the wind could carry away the stink of cat and blood and death.

Then she leaned against a bundle of supplies, reloading her flintlock, and resumed waiting. Though she was shaking inside, her hands were steady, and Judith felt that she had done fairly well, considering her adversary. Tomorrow, she was determined, they would skin the panther and scrub the hide with ashes.

It would make a fine blanket for the baby.

* * * * * * *

When David and Joseph returned, leading Jess, both of them were soaked and shivering. All was in order. The rain had slacked to a steady drizzle, and the small shelter no longer stank of blood. However, when the men stumbled over the carcass of the panther outside, their reaction was surprising.

"You'd think I was going to sit here and let that beast eat the baby," she said at last, when they were done exclaiming and measuring and checking the darkness for any other predator that might stalk the camp.

David had the grace to blush in the light of the rekindled lantern, and Joseph turned his attention to his new child. Cassie, weak but able to grin at her husband, held the little one in the crook of her arm.

Judith knew it was worth everything to see Joseph's dark face crease into a smile as he stared down at his daughter.

"We'll rest here for a bit," David told him. "We want to skin out that cat, and Cassie needs the sleep; to be honest, so do I. It isn't every day we face this sort of thing.

"Besides, the storm has to have softened up the ground, and the last farmer I talked to said that up ahead it's all low country. Best let the water go down before we cross it."

Judith breathed a sigh of relief. She was weary all the way down to her bones, it seemed as if; even her hair was tired feeling, when she let down the thick coil that had tangled around the edges until it was almost impossible to run her brush through it.

They had built a fire outside the shelter as soon as the rain stopped. It was shedding its own red light to join that of the lantern, and as she let down her hair, the auburn coils caught the light and sparked with red.

David crawled around behind her and touched it gently, "I never saw anything like that!" he murmured. "I've known you all my life, but I never saw you with your hair down. Could I...could I brush it for you?"

"Oh, David, would you?" she asked. "I'm so tired, and it's so heavy and hard to manage. When I sit down it trails off on the ground, and if I stand up I'll have to get out in the rain and bend double to get to the ends."

As he carefully untangled the knots and smoothed the long strands, she closed her eyes and sighed. Not even her mother had ever helped her with such a task. A husband who cared enough to do this for her was something she had never dreamed of having. Medlar would certainly never have thought of it, and if he had she wouldn't have wanted him doing it.

As David brushed out the long locks and spoke softly, she drifted off to sleep, and for some reason she did not dream of the bright eyes of the panther or of the faceless tracker who might be on their trail. Instead, she dreamed of bright things, shapeless but beckoning, that lay in the future they would share in a new country.

BORN REBEL

CHAPTER SIX

THE NATCHEZ TRACE—JUDITH MCCARRAN

The third morning dawned clear and bright enough to promise that the damp country ahead must have dried out to some extent. The panther skin Judith had scraped and rubbed with ashes was rolled and tied behind Joseph's saddle, waiting for a time when they could cure it properly.

As soon as they ate a bite and drank scalding cups of coffee, Judith found herself on the trail once more, her back aching. Her stomach felt queasy, but that might, she hoped, be blamed on the stress of the past days.

Cassie and the baby seemed strong, and the infant suckled well. Judith, remembering her Mama's needs, made sure they carried plenty of water, for the baby would pull a lot of liquid from her mother and it had to be replenished. On the move, without livestock at hand, there was no way to supplement the child's food supply, so they must take care to safeguard the mother.

David had been right about the low country ahead. Water stood in every low spot, and even the pine flats had their feet in deep mud. The many creeks they had to cross were bank-full, and logs, bushes, and any rock thrust above the surrounding water tended to be full of angry water moccasins and turtles.

By the time they found what they were sure must be the Natchez Trace, Judith was all but exhausted. In addition, she had begun to feel even more queasy in the mornings. She was almost sure, by now, that she might be pregnant, although there had not been time to become completely certain.

She said nothing to David. He had enough to worry about, she felt, for they came upon more and more indications that other travelers followed the Trace. Everyone knew that those who became entangled with the law or with feuds back in the east often took this route to the wild Texas country, and unfortunately they didn't leave their criminal habits behind.

Though she kept her ears trained on all the sounds in the forest around them, Judith now knew that unexpected dangers could come out of those tangled thickets and towering trees. David rode behind with his musket ready and his knife at hand, while Joseph, leading the way, kept turning his head from side to side, watching for any sign of trouble.

Night was the worst time of all, for though the days on the tunnel-like trail were tense, darkness hid even more dangers than did the shadows of the ancient trees. Whippoorwills wailed, owls hooted or quivered wavering cries overhead, and far-off howls spoke of red wolves hunting for prey. In that medley of noises, the approach of stealthy feet could easily be missed by even the most alert ear.

They were moving along a crooked stretch, one afternoon, with Joseph already out of sight beyond a bend ahead and David hidden by the thick trunks of overarching trees behind. Judith saw sudden movement before she heard the yipping cry of the marauders who came out of the forest on foot.

"David!" she cried, pulling her horse around beside Cassie's and priming her flintlock. The first man reached her just as she had the weapon ready, and she blew a hole into his head through the top of his hat. He dropped instantly, but another was upon her.

She was flailing with her knife, and Cassie was holding the baby in one arm, the skinning knife in her other hand, doing her best to fight off their attackers. Then David was there, riding into the huddle of men and knocking them like skittles into the trees.

Joseph arrived almost as quickly, and between them the two beat back the six men who had thought to find this an easy mark. Two broke for the deeper forest, but David's musket brought one down and Joseph's knife flew with unerring accuracy to skewer the other.

That left them with two dead or dying men, one of them the man Judith had shot and the other one whom Cassie had cut so deeply that he would soon bleed to death. The remaining pair seemed to have lost any will to fight. Running seemed to be their goal, though the fate of the first two runners had damped their enthusiasm.

"We ought to hang them right here," David said. Judith knew he was right, but she also knew her husband. He had not been reared to kill men needlessly, and he would not do it now.

"Why don't we disarm them, take their boots, and tie them to a tree, though not so tightly that they cannot free themselves if they work hard and long?" she asked. "It will, if nothing else, give them time to think about their erring ways."

David's expression lightened. He had been prepared to string them up to one of the Spanish moss-laden oak branches, and she knew he would have struggled with his conscience for days and weeks afterward. She had, after all, known him since they were children.

If it had been left to her, she would have shot the raiders where they stood and left them for the crows, but she said nothing about that. It was too soon to let her husband see the cold steel at the core of the woman he had married.

He still thought of her as gentle and loving; though she was growing very fond of him, that feeling did not extend to would-be murderers.

With great caution, her small troop traveled the winding tunnel under even more tremendous oak trees. It took days of riding and walking through the sodden countryside to reach the high bluff beside the great Mississippi.

There a huddle of houses and a few shops marked the site of Natchez, where one could find a ferry across the wide river. It was not a very large town, despite being the capital of Mississippi, but Judith had grown up beyond reach of any town at all. To her it seemed vast, and she looked about her with awe as they rode down the muddy street.

They passed the old fort, built by the French, a man told David when they asked for directions. It commanded the river below, and Judith thought that anyone trying to attack the town from the west would be in very bad trouble. You could just about stop an army by rolling rocks down on its troops.

The place stunk of pigs, river, and privies, but as they approached the bluff overlooking the stream she could see the shops and shanties far below, built along the shelf of land that served as a beach at river level. The crude log ferry was tied up to a deep-set post, its stern downstream, its roughly pointed nose bobbing with every wave of the passing current.

The river was high from the recent heavy rains, and its brown waters lapped at the levee protecting the lower town. Even as she looked, the drowned carcass of a horse came down the current.

She turned to David, feeling a surge of joy. "Once we get over there..."—she pointed to the other side of the brown water—"...we might be safe, don't you think? Surely nobody will follow us so far."

David looked down at her, with worry lines between

his eyes. "Joseph still feels something coming," he said. "And I do too. But maybe once we're over in the Louisiana country that will change."

Judith sighed. She had hoped, by now, to feel secure, beyond the reach of Oscar Medlar or any henchman he might send. Yet tomorrow they might cross the river on that frail-looking ferry, and then...oh surely no one would still pursue them.

* * * * * *

They camped for the night beyond the town, in the edge of the forest. She and David and Joseph took turns standing guard through the hours of darkness, for riffraff of every stripe found a haven here.

Even at a distance of a mile, they could hear shouts and raucous laughter from the shanties under the bluff. Judith wondered if those who were to work the ferry across the river tomorrow were among the drunken revelers. All they possessed rode with them on their horses. Anything lost would be hard to replace, even if they spent some of their small store of gold.

Once, while Joseph watched, there was a sharp crack among the trees, as if someone had stepped on a fallen branch. All the adults were awake at once, hands on their weapons, but after half an hour there was no further disturbance, and Joseph motioned for them to go back to sleep.

Cassie's baby did not cry. She had tried to, once or twice at tense moments, and the young woman had held the infant's nose until she stopped heaving with effort. When Judith protested, the girl shook her head.

"It's no good if she gets us all kilt," she said. "My grampa tell me that back in the old place over the sea there's lots of dangerous animals and tribes that makes war. Babies don't be let to cry. It's too dangerous."

"But she might smother!" Judith said, peering down at the small face that no longer was showing signs of tears.

"She got her mouth. When she breathe through that, she sho' can't cry out loud," the child's mother said, and Judith had to admit that was true.

* * * * * * *

When a mockingbird tuned up in the big oaks over the camp, Judith was already awake, packing up the small items used the night before. David and Joseph had the horses saddled, the pack animal loaded. It was time to cross the Big River, and the thought made her shiver with anticipation.

Flimsy as the ferry looked, the thought that some agent of Oscar Medlar might be dogging her footsteps made the risk of crossing the river seem far preferable to standing still and facing someone sent by her would-be bridegroom. And if, as Joseph thought, that agent might be Jonas Bluth...she shuddered, this time with revulsion.

A nasty animal, that one. She had seen the results of his work when he brought back runaway slaves; those she saw had been bleeding from multiple whip marks and raw with contusions from beatings with the big man's fists. Man or woman or child, he all but killed them, stopping just short of losing his fee for catching them.

She shook off the thought and led Jess after Cassie. Now the girl was able to walk without any problem, though she hung the infant in a bag on the saddle, where the young one had begun to laugh and blow bubbles and even smile, when someone paused to play with her.

There was no time for that this morning, though Judith often paced beside the gelding Cassie rode, her finger clasped in the child's warm, damp ones. Today they moved fast, riding once they cleared the brush and trees, through the muddy streets, the throngs of shoppers and sellers, toward the road leading down the face of the bluff to the waiting ferry.

"How do you keep the thing from floating away downstream?" she asked a bearded fellow who was helping them get their animals aboard.

"Look up there," he said, pointing to the top of the cliff.

She saw, after some effort, a thin dark line extending downward at a long angle toward the distant Louisiana shore.

"That's a heavy rope. They replace it every few weeks, what with the strain and the wet and the mildew. The ferry travels along it, though sometimes when the river's up like this I wonder if it's going to hold. So far it has." He grinned, a snaggle of brown-yellow teeth, and spat over the side into the eddying water.

"Thank you," Judith murmured. She wondered how anyone had managed to get such a line across the river, which was wider than any she had ever seen. Then, realizing that they and all their possessions would be entrusted to that frail strand, she wondered if it would make this trip.

The river, at this level, rushed past like a great brown beast, struggling to free itself from its banks. While she watched, it broke off a chunk of the bluff upstream and carried it in a boil of mud past the dancing ferry.

"This is better than being married to Oscar Medlar," Judith said aloud, gripping the stirrup, both to comfort Jess and to ease her own fear. "Even if we drown on the way, this is better."

David, just ahead of her, gentling his own mount, turned and smiled. "We'll make it," he said. "You just watch."

Just then the ferryman loosed the tether, and the ferry swung instantly into the current, straining to follow the impulse to go downstream. The huge rope fastened to its bow tightened, and the craft moved in a great arc from the dock behind to the low, tree-covered bank ahead. How the ferrymen managed to control their direction Judith could not see, for she had her eyes shut as tightly as possible.

When she opened them again, the dock was moving closer, and the tug of the river seemed less, probably because on this side there was a point of land extending into the stream and protecting the landing from the worst of the current.

Jess stamped and whinnied, not liking this kind of travel any more than Judith did. Patting the mare's neck, .Judith spoke softly to her, and she quieted. Then the ferry shuddered as it made contact with the eastern dock, and the ferryman's helper jumped ashore to drop the anchor loop over a bollard.

She heard Cassie's small gasp of relief as the craft came to a stop or at least stopped moving over the river.

It still danced underfoot as they made their way carefully down the ramp and onto the doubtful security of the rude landing.

"We're over the river," she called to David. "Maybe...."

He grinned at her, also relieved, but a hint of worry still lived behind his eyes. They would go as if danger walked just behind them, she knew. It was better not to be surprised by anything, on such a journey as theirs.

BORN REBEL

CHAPTER SEVEN

PINE WOODS

There was a scroungy sort of town that had grown up at the western end of the ferry. Even scroungier people lolled about, leaning against mossy posts and spitting streams of tobacco juice as near the feet of passersby as they felt it safe to do. David felt uncomfortable with having women in his party as he squashed through the mud along the road leading away from the dock, feeling hostile eyes blazing from narrow, bearded faces.

The place stank of water moccasins, wet pine needles, and unwashed people. He wrinkled his nose and glanced back at Judith, who studiously kept her attention fixed on him and tried to smile as their eyes met. She was a bright girl, his wife. Even without knowing anything about such human filth as this, her instinct told her not to meet the gazes of any of the men along the way.

Cassie hunched into her shawl, holding the baby close and avoiding even looking at Joseph. He, too, walked silently, watching the horses, avoiding any notice of the watchers along the way. David had known the slave all his life, and he understood that Joseph knew their peril. Thieves and murderers, running from crimes back home in the East, haunted such places, to which travelers must come if they wanted to cross the river. They would steal anything, from gold to people, given the chance.

Turning to watch the road ahead, David kept his musket in hand and saw to it that his big knife was in clear view at his side. It wouldn't do to allow these men to think his people were easy prey.

The splop of hooves in mud came steadily behind him, and now he kept his face turned toward the pine forest that loomed to the west of the pile of spilled garbage that was the town. Only when he moved under the outermost branches did he draw an easier breath.

"We'll turn off on the first path we see that goes in the right direction," he murmured to Judith, who had moved forward until she was at his elbow. "We don't need to stay on the main trail. I wouldn't trust a one of those ragtags not to cut our throats in our sleep, if they got the chance."

"Or worse," she said, and he knew she had understood their danger as well as he. For a woman there were worse things than being killed in her sleep.

But after all he didn't take the first or even the second trail that forked from the main road westward. That would have been too obvious, if anyone followed them. He watched carefully as the day waned and a brisk wind rose to whistle through the needles of the pines.

They moved between scraps of cleared land, from time to time, but the wet year had obviously drowned any crop sowed in spring. Log cabins had stood on two of the farms, but they seemed abandoned, possibly to the flooding. High water marks rose to the third log on one of them.

The country seemed deserted, but David had a good notion that they were being watched from hidden coverts as they passed; he felt that no horse or bag or person in his troop was overlooked. That was why, once they were deep in the forest again, he turned off between two overgrown pine trees into the wood itself, trusting to the deep mat of pine needles to hide the tracks of their horses.

The pines were tremendous, rising some forty or fifty

feet before thrusting out a lateral branch. Below, the needles made a carpet heavy enough to silence even the horses' hooves. So dense was the greenery above that few bushes or even low-growing vines cluttered the forest floor.

Except for the shrill calls of a jay and a distant caw from an occasional patrolling crow, it was almost silent as they moved down the great nave of trees into the depths of the wood. It was also very dark there, with the sky shut away beyond a roof of black-green pine tops.

David knew they must camp soon or move blindly through unfamiliar country. Only when it became really dangerous to keep on did he call a halt in a hollow among big pines and hickories.

"No fire tonight," he said, as Judith and Joseph helped him unload the beasts. "We'll stand watch two at a time, first Joseph and Judith, then Cassie and me, and we'll keep an ear open even when we take our turns resting.

"I talked to a man in Natchez who told me that a lot of those who take the ferry west never are heard of again. From the look of the dockside folks back there in Vidalia, I'm not surprised. They're likely moving after us right now."

Joseph helped his wife spread the tarpaulin and smooth blankets beneath it. The breeze was now filled with moisture, and it was clear they might expect a shower before daylight.

When they were done, Joseph moved to stand beside David. "I don't like the looks of this country. Looks even snakier than the places we been. And the snakes is the nice folks. The human bein' snakes is worse'n the ones that got no legs."

David laughed, relieved to find he still could. Judith and Cassie joined him, and for a moment there was a ring of human warmth there in the dark space among the pines. Then Judith opened the pack of food and shared out raw bacon, cornpone they had baked while camped in Natchez, and fruit he had bought from a peddler.

Judith took the musket, not even fumbling in the darkness, and she and Joseph moved to opposite sides of their small clearing. David felt for his knife, freed it from its sheath, and stretched himself in his blankets, leaving the shelter for Cassie and the baby. In two minutes he was fast asleep.

When he woke he could see a pale mist of moonlight sifting down through the branches. Judith's hand was on his arm, shaking gently. "Time, husband. The moon is overhead, and most of the clouds seem to have blown away. Maybe we won't get a rain tonight."

"Pray we do," he told her. "Rain washes out tracks."

Yawning, he took his place, hearing Cassie settling herself in the hidden nook between oak roots that he and Joseph had chosen for her. Although she had not fully recovered from the birth, the girl didn't lack courage; he knew she would give warning in good time. Her eyes were sharp, and she was becoming a more accurate shot, when they had time for her to practice with the spare musket.

David sat with his back to a rough-barked trunk, his legs folded Indian style and his musket primed and ready. It was so dark beneath the canopy of needled crests that even the misted moon above them could do little to relieve the blackness.

That was good. Though he could see nothing, anyone trying to follow their trail could certainly manage to do no more.

Straining to see was futile. He closed his eyes and listened intently, sorting out the night sounds of hunting animals from the trills of mockingbirds sitting high above in the moonlight. A mournful cry in the distance told him a red wolf was calling to his pack, and a gruff snarling nearer at hand spoke of bobcats quarrelling over a kill.

The gunshot made him open his eyes again, rising to

hear better. It was far away, and he thought it came from the road they had left behind. Had someone followed them, only to tangle with someone else from one of the farms, who also intended to rob the travelers? There was no way of knowing.

Joseph had checked their track, after the horses passed, removing dung and smoothing out disturbed patches of pine needles. Surely sloppy villains like those in Vidalia couldn't find where his group turned off the main trail. Particularly not in the dark. Those who had watched them might, though he doubted it.

David sighed, shaking his head. Some things could never be known, but it was frustrating to wonder without any hope of learning what was going on. Still, he had learned the hard way that life was like that, and there was nothing to do but go ahead with your own business and let the rest go hang.

The slivers of pale sky darkened as the moon went down the west. Occasionally he could hear a snore from Joseph or a sigh from Judith. Cassie was silent, and he wondered if she had fallen asleep.

Then he heard a whimper from the baby, and she slipped across to the shelter. Soon contented gurgles told him she was nursing her daughter. He should have known. New mothers had ears that missed nothing. In a bit she settled the sleepy infant back in its nest beside Judith and crept back to her post.

David smiled. He knew a lot of people back home who discounted women and blacks as equally worthless except for having babies and working in the fields. He wouldn't have swapped his wife and Joseph and Cassie for a whole troop of the red-necked idiots who were better at drinking and bragging than anything else.

Already his companions had proved their worth in a scrap. He was learning it could be a good thing for enemies to underestimate you. That tended to make them careless.

A fallen branch crackled, off to his left. Had someone taken an incautious step? Or had a browsing deer or roaming cougar crossed it?

A screech owl began to quaver right above him and almost made him jump out of his skin. The creature spoke three times before taking off in an almost soundless rush of air through ruffled feathers, and David knew something had disturbed it as it sat digesting its nightly ration of mice or small birds.

He flattened to the mat of needles and slithered toward the spot where the branch had cracked, pausing frequently to listen. He found that when he looked upward, shapes ahead of him were silhouetted against the tiny patches of paler sky, so when he located the cause of the disturbance he had no trouble in identifying it.

A black bear ambled across his route, stopping to sniff the air. Now why was he out at night? Nothing bothered bears as they scrounged for food by day, so it was a good bet something had disturbed the creature at rest. He seemed to be heading away from the road, which David estimated wound along from east to west some three or four miles distant.

It was a good bet someone was moving on the road, and the critters were moving away from it because of that. Good thing they'd cut away from the main trail, he thought. If they'd stayed on it, they might be right in the middle of whatever was going on.

He eased backward, as soon as the bear moved on, and resumed his watch while the sky paled and night drew away among the giant trees. Another mockingbird tuned up, and its repertoire of borrowed calls waked his companions. He heard Joseph cough and spit; Judith gave the small grunt he had come to know and sat up.

"All well," he said in a voice aimed to travel no farther then his listeners. "We'd better move. I think somebody's back there on the road, and there's no guarantee they'll miss the place where we turned off."

Cassie came out of her hiding place and fed the baby again while they packed the loads onto the horses. Then, chewing on cornpone, they headed west again, guided by the slanting rays of the rising sun that struck through the canopy of branches.

Joseph came behind, as usual, making as sure as possible that they left no plain track for any bandit to follow. Only after they crossed many miles that included two big creeks, bank full and very swift for lowland streams, did David call a halt and risk building a cookfire.

Joseph pulled from his pack two possums he had killed with a stick the evening before. The stupid animals, crossing their trail, had played dead, and that was all the opportunity any experienced possum hunter needed.

Possum was a staple, back home, and they spitted them on sticks and roasted them over the fire, reveling in the drip of fat into the coals and the smell of cooking meat. It was time they had cooked food, David knew, for they needed to sustain their strength in this mosquito-ridden country, where they could expect to come down with fever before long.

Sickness was a thing to be feared, and he had no intention of neglecting anything that might help his people avoid that. When they all sat about the remnant of the fire, grease dripping from hands and faces, he felt reassured.

They were all healthy people, even Cassie, who seemed to be recovering nicely. Fed well and rested from time to time, surely they could all make it to the Sabine River and their new home in Texas.

He felt his heart speed up when he thought of that good soil, the big timber he had heard about, the wide spaces that were uninhabited except by occasional Indians. He glanced aside at his wife, and she smiled. Sometimes he thought she could read his thoughts, for he felt the same excitement in her grip as she took his hand and squeezed it.

Only a matter of days now lay between their present position and that new home. Even as he thought it, there came a rumble of thunder, and rain began to patter overhead on leaves and pine needles, coming through like drips through a leaky roof.

"Damn!" said David, rising to kick out the fire and cover it with ash and dead leaves. "Looks as if we have to travel wet for a while."

He was right. It rained steadily, sometimes flooding down so hard they had to halt and huddle against the horses beneath the huge pines, sometimes just pattering through the canopy above. It was miserable traveling, but nobody complained.

He knew they had all heard that gunshot in the night. He had told them about the bear. Rain or not, they were lucky still to be on their way, alive and uninjured.

BORN REBEL

CHAPTER EIGHT

A DAMN HARD TRAIL TO FOLLOW—
JONAS BLUTH

Jonas climbed onto Mossback for the tenth time in two hours. There was just no way to know if this batch of riders was the right one or not.

In the past weeks he'd only lucked out once, and that was when he located McCarran's cousin. Though the man and his wife played dumb, there were others in the Settlement, and Jonas had learned for certain that the runaways had been married by a preacher. At the time he'd thought that was the best thing, because it gave him leave to kill the whole crew.

Now he was wondering if these might be the only blots on his record. He'd followed them pretty well as long as they stuck to the main trail westward, but suddenly they seemed to disappear off the face of the earth. He'd backtracked, talked to long-boned men working in skimpy fields, questioned crippled grandmas who could only sit on their porches and card out cottonseeds or shell beans. After a certain point along the route, nobody had seen his quarry.

He decided at last just to head for Natchez, which was

the nearest crossing over the Mississippi. They'd have to use a ferry someplace, and it was too far through terrible swampy country to make it to New Orleans. Greenville was way out of the route, too far to the north.

Sure enough, once he reached the riverside town he found idlers who would have seen anything coming through. He camped in the forest outside town, rested a bit, and proceeded on foot to the dock below the bluff, mixing easily with the lowlifes who lounged there. Two in particular caught his fancy.

He ambled along and came to a stop beside the dock, where they seemed to have taken root. Sticking out his hand, he said, "Name's Jonas Bluth. Just come in from Ca'lina. Looks like you fellows pretty well know the place."

The taller man squinted at him, his pale eyes narrow with suspicion. "Crom Bidwell," he muttered, without shaking hands. "This here's Amos Clark. We keep an eye out, sure nuff."

Jonas gazed out over the muddy river and sighed. "I bet my folks done gone across," he muttered. "I knowed I was late, but I never thought they'd beat me here. They promised to camp and wait, but I know old David; he's always in an almighty hurry."

"Lookin' for somebody?" Clark asked. "If they've crossed here, it's sure and certain we've seen 'em. How many and what'd they look like?"

Bluth didn't smile, though he felt like it. "Why, if you'll come into the saloon and let me buy you a glass of rotgut, I'll tell you all about it."

Clark nodded, and Bidwell moved at once toward the shanty toward which Bluth pointed. Jonas followed them into the dark interior, which stank of alcohol, piss, and vomit. He clinked coins onto the counter, and the black barman poured three skimpy glasses of dark stuff that came near to smelling worse than the inside of the saloon.

Cramped into a corner at a shackledy table, Jonas put his drink in front of him and stared through the gloom at his companions. "You got to know that my sister's gone and married against our folks's wishes. She and her new husband, David McCarran, and two slaves taken off for Texas about a month and a half ago.

"They ought to be here waitin' for me, but David's always in a hurry. I'd bet anything they've already crossed, leavin' me to catch up any way I can."

Bidwell cocked his head. "What's she look like, this sister of yourn?"

Jonas knew the man didn't believe a word he'd said, but he'd react if he had seen the group. "She's tall, for a woman. Slender, lots of kind of red-brown hair and big gray eyes. Not a bit like me, of course. Just my half sister, in fact.

"David's not much taller'n she is, wiry, with blue eyes and brown hair. His slave's a bit older than he is, big fellow with a scar on his arm. There's a woman slave, too. Couple of extra horses. You seen 'em?"

Clark slanted his eyes at Bidwell, who looked noncommittal. "Lots of folks cross here every time the ferry runs. Last run was how long, Amos? Three-four days?"

"Nearer a week," Clark replied. "Not been so many folks crossing these days, count of the floods back east a ways. Takes a while to wait for a full load."

Bluth knew he had to play them like bass on a line, not too hard and not too gentle. Now he had to find out what they knew without spending too much of the money Oscar had given him.

He sighed. "I guess it'll be a while before the ferry crosses again? I'd be willing to pay for a special trip, if they've already gone, but I can't waste the money if they ain't. Might even spare a bit for anybody that helped me get on my way.

"Haven't got much, but my sister's dependin' on me to

come with 'em." These bastards would kill you for the lint in your pocket, he knew, but he was confident of his own strength and cunning.

Bidwell looked deeply into his glass of river water whiskey. "How much you pay?" he asked. "I think we may've seen 'em."

"Already crossed?"

"Two trips past. Mebbe ten days? Near two weeks, it may be. You must of got stuck in the high water."

Clark piped up, "Couldn't miss that high-headed woman. Stepped right along like she felt good as any man and better than some. Will that fellow she married take her down a peg?"

"I doubt it. He's soft, always was. But they're married now, so if she puts a ring in his nose, that's his own look-out," Bluth said. "I promised her I'd come, and come I will, if you fellows'll see if we can make up a load for the ferry. I 'spect it would cross if it had a pretty good bunch wanting to go."

It cost him three dollars to make up the load for the ferry and another half dollar to pay for himself and his horse. If McCarran was almost two weeks ahead of him, the trail would be cold, even on this sparsely traveled route.

Once across, he might find more of the ilk of Bidwell and Clark to aim him in the right direction, but somehow he didn't feel confident of that. The hangers-on around the ferry seemed the kind to rob you if they could, kill you if necessary, and forget about you as soon as possible.

* * * * * * *

Vidalia was so small and so sorry that even Bluth found it disgusting. Nobody there admitted seeing anyone, white or black, male or female, cross on the ferry, ever. That told him someone among the hangdog bunch had maybe tried to rob them and failed. It also told him that McCarran, even burdened with two women and a black, might be a more formidable adversary than he had suspected.

Thinking about that, Bluth rode west along the muddy track that wound among heavy pine forest, crossed even muddier creeks and bogs, and showed only animal tracks left since the last heavy rains. If his quarry had passed here, there was no sign of it.

He felt unseen eyes watching him as he passed the cabins built on hardscrabble farms. Knowing too well the ways of bushwhackers, Bluth kept his weapons ready and his eyes peeled for trouble. That was why he noticed the patch of dried brown blood staining the mud of the track.

"Damn!" He swung down from the saddle and examined the trampled spot closely. Even the rain of the past weeks had not entirely washed away the dark stain, and when he sniffed cautiously he smelled the distant taint of death. Somebody or something had died right here, and he didn't think it was an animal.

Drat the luck! He had to know who it was. If it was McCarran or the slave or Judith, it was best to know right now and be done with it.

Even after so long, the faint reek still guided him as he followed his nose into the tangle of undergrowth edging the track. Beyond that the forest floor was smoothly carpeted with pine needles, but something had been dragged through them. The needles were still disarranged, sticking up haphazardly to form a distinct trail.

He catfooted it along the way, winding among the big trees. The track ended on a creek bank, where it was plain something had been tumbled over the muddy bank. A scrap of cloth still hung onto a bramble growing out of the bank.

Cursing, Bluth slipped and slid down the red mud slope, to find a body piled up against a clump of willows at the bottom. It was half submerged, but the trees had held it in place, though there had obviously been high water not too long before.

A man, it was clear from the clothing. That was good. Bluth had plans for Judith. He poked the thing over with a long stick and stared at what was left of the face. Then he sighed. It was plainly not David McCarran nor yet his man slave.

Though it was impossible to tell what this one had looked like, the hair was the wrong color, long and coal black, and the bared teeth were missing three in front and a couple at the back. This had been an older man than either male in the McCarran party.

Bluth wondered if McCarran had killed him, or if two would-be bushwhacker groups had tangled while trailing common quarry. He'd never know.

He turned and tramped back to the spot where he'd tied Mossback. There he took out the map he'd finagled out of Bidwell, over in Natchez. There were several ways to cross the Sabine River into Texas, and Bidwell and Clark had made a bit of cash by keeping badly drawn maps up-to-date, using the information they gleaned from the few who returned eastward from Texas.

Shreve's Port was considerably north of the most direct route west, and Bluth knew David McCarran well enough to understand that he wouldn't waste travel time, so near his goal. No, the last word his informants had marked on the map was that there was a ferry on a direct route from Vidalia, straight along the Camino Real. Gaines was the name scrawled there.

On the east side of the Sabine the mapmakers had carefully printed, NO MAN'S LAND. GOOD PICKINGS. This was, they had told Bluth, the area used as a buffer zone between the Texas Territory of Spain and the United States, after the purchase of the Louisiana Territory from France. It sounded good to Jonas Bluth, who liked nothing better than a place where no law was in force.

He had no fear of bad'uns who might roost there. He felt himself the equal of any and much harder than most.

After studying the map for several minutes, he decided that, given the lead they had, he would be wiser to head straight for that ferry, as fast as Mossback could travel without doing him major damage. If they had cut off the trail again they would almost certainly be delayed by high water and heavy mud and crossings over flooded creeks. He could catch up some time by going the direct route.

He led Mossback to the bloodstained mud patch, looked down and grinned. He was still in business.

When he rode westward, he could almost hear sighs of relief from the concealing thickets beyond the track. Those bastards better take care how they watched him. He was meaner than any of 'em and smarter, too. Nobody bushwhacked Jonas Bluth.

BORN REBEL

CHAPTER NINE

JUDITH MCCARRAN

Judith had never dreamed, when she flung her hat over the windmill and ran away with David, that her life could ever become harder than it had been at home. Now she knew. Not only was the road west incredibly difficult, the mud bottomless, the creeks raging with brown foam and angry cottonmouth moccasins, but she had learned about morning sickness in the hardest way possible.

She walked too far every day, dropping onto her blankets at night with a groan, muscles cramping. Earlier in the journey they had ridden for miles at a stretch. Now, in this wet and sticky country, even the horses had a hard time getting themselves through the miry spots and boggy creeks that seemed to appear at the bottom of every ridge. Their riders had to make it on their own.

She had left a trail of vomit, she felt sure, that even a blind man could follow by the smell. Though she knew Joseph came behind, trying to clear their trail, it didn't comfort her to know that he still felt someone was following persistently. The thought made her feel even more clammy and sick than she would have if they had simply been traveling through this awful country.

At last she became so ill that even David, driven as he

was to reach his goal, knew they must stop to let her rest. Cassie, too, was exhausted, drained by nursing and tending the baby, and Joseph was looking very thin and stringy.

After the warnings they had heard about the lawless zone east of the Sabine, they hesitated to go forward and make a camp there. David consulted with Joseph, and they stopped in heavy pine timber along a ridge overlooking the Arroyo Hondo. One of the great trees had fallen to some recent windstorm, its roots heaving up and leaving a deep hole sheltered on the west by the root ball.

It was raining again, a dismal drizzle that pattered on the tarpaulin they strung over the depression. Joseph piled pine needles deeply in the cup, covering the mud and cushioning their bones, while David built a tiny fire on the raw earth just beyond their shelter.

"We'll all get sick if we stay wet," he said, and Judith agreed. Already she was coughing and sneezing, even in the sticky heat of summer. They put on dry clothing from their packs and strung the damp bits and pieces beside the fire.

Then David went silently into the pines, and Judith knew he would be watching until relieved by Joseph. The one thing, she realized, that made women unequal to men was childbearing. The sickness and stress of pregnancy and the infinite care to be taken with an infant bore heavily upon her and Cassie.

She turned on her side and stared out from beneath the tarpaulin. The thin smoke from the little fire drifted away downwind through the trees, and she hoped it would attract no attention from undesirables. If it did, she would rise and fight, but the thought made her quease.

She had been able, before she became pregnant, to outwork any man in the cotton fields, so it was not being female that was the problem. No, men had a surefire way of destroying one's strength and stamina, although she knew they were unaware that was the result of their enthusiastic activities.

Many times she had heard her father curse her mother for fainting in the fields. Now she understood her mother's wretched state, for every time that happened she had been carrying a child. Too late, Judith grieved for the woman who had given birth to her; she resented the heavy-handed father who had intended to sentence her to the same kind of miserable life.

She was lucky David was considerate, where Pa had been harsh and unbending, expecting the same amount of work from a pregnant wife as he got from a strong young daughter or himself. If you had to be female, she decided, it was better to be hooked up with a caring man.

Oscar Medlar—she shuddered at the thought—would have worked her to death, pregnant or not. Or she might have killed him, if he drove her too far, and she would have been hanged. Men might kill women with impunity, but the law didn't allow for the opposite to happen without punishment.

Then she was asleep, and only when Cassie shook her shoulder to offer her food did she wake again. She was not hungry, her rebellious stomach heaving at the thought of swallowing anything. Yet she knew, for the sake of the child she carried, she must force something down.

Cornbread was terrible to throw up, as rough and gritty coming up as it was going down. Meat was just as bad. But Cassie had managed to boil a bit of squirrel in their pot to make broth. That went down more easily, and it seemed willing to stay in her stomach, this time.

Then she slept again, and when she came fully to herself at last, two days had passed. She felt better than she had in weeks, and the smell of rabbit stew bubbling in the pot made her stomach growl with hunger. Perhaps, after all, she was going to live to see Texas.

The rain had stopped while she slept, and the ground below the ridge was steaming with summer heat. She sat with her back to the tree trunk as she ate, staring across the bottomlands that flanked the river they must cross. It was hard to believe that down there in the rich green forest were men who lived like beasts, waiting to kill anyone who came through in order to steal whatever they carried.

She dreaded traveling over that dangerous ground, but once they passed beyond and crossed the river they would be in Texas. Thinking of the land they might buy or claim there made her shiver with delight. Despite her father's harshness, Judith had always loved farming. Now she and David would be free to do it in their own time and their own way.

They waited until she had recovered a bit and Cassie and the baby seemed fit. Then, very early one morning, when dawn was only a promise in the east, David led their line of horses and walkers away through the huge pine trees. They went a long way before sunrise, and when they camped at last it was beside the river they had sought for so long.

The Sabine, its water muddy yellow-brown, moved lazily between overgrown banks, where willows and oaks and sweetgum trees bent their gnarled backs over the crooked stream. Cattails grew in profusion in the shallow edges of its many loops and bends, and fish plopped loudly, feeding in the twilight.

As Judith watched the darkening waters, she saw a swirl of movement, twin bubbles moving against the current. A moccasin, swimming across the river, was leaving behind a V-shaped wake, but even as she wondered what the bubbles might be there came a snap, and the snake disappeared into the jaws of an alligator. She shuddered and turned toward David, who had also been watching.

"We'll have to teach the baby to be careful of critters," he said, but his hand crept out to find hers and gave it a squeeze.

She leaned against him, and the mellow fish, mud, and

water smell of the river filled her nostrils. Pine tanged the air as well, and the smoke from their cook fire laced its own aroma through the others.

Again Judith shivered, but this time it was with anticipation. The new life was about to begin. Tomorrow they would move along the river to find the ferry, and then... and then they would step upon the soil of this new country where they would live out their lives and rear their children.

* * * * * * *

Here, too, it had been raining, as it had farther east. The river was high, its current boiling about snags and logjams, frills of yellow foam collecting along the fringes of water weeds. They moved upstream, for David had calculated their point of arrival as being somewhat below the site of the ferry.

"The letter says a Mr. James Gaines runs the ferry, and he's a good man. Beyond that, though, it's still pretty wild country, and some dangerous people may have settled there. We have to go carefully," he warned his people, and Judith could hear the unease in his voice.

There was a clump of log shelters on the eastern bank of the Sabine, when they arrived at the ferry site. The craft itself was tied to a big post sunk into the shallows beside a rude wharf; its stern was downstream, its bow bobbing violently in the flooded current. As she led her horse behind David into the open space beside the wharf, she realized that a group of silent men stood there, too, staring at the ferry and the river.

David handed her the reins of his own mount and moved up beside a big fellow in a wide hat. "Is it too rough to cross?" he asked.

"Unh!" the man grunted. "Look at it, man! It'd break the cable and carry the ferry away down to the Gulf of

Mexico."

Judith, just behind them, realized he was right. The thick hemp cable might be the size of her own waist, but a loaded ferry might well overload even its capacity. While she stood watching, the swollen body of a cow came down the flood, bumped into the blunt prow of the ferry, and swirled away downstream. She had no desire to join it on its journey.

She tugged at David's sleeve. "Let's camp until the water goes down," she whispered into his ear when he leaned toward her.

He nodded. "We'll camp until Mr. Gaines decides it's safe to cross," he told the man. "I want to talk to him, though. Where might I find him?"

"He's in his cabin that he uses on this side of the river, when he can't get back home. That'un there." The fellow gestured toward the least flimsy of the shelters, and David turned toward it.

"Find us a good camp site," he said to Judith. "I'll come when I've talked to the ferryman."

The river bank was low, wet, and overgrown with tangles of button willow, yaupon, and blackberry vines. Judith didn't want to be so near the water anyway, for if it rose, she could see that the levels had, in the past, come higher than the level of the shanty. She'd seen enough dangers so far without courting more.

Joseph went scouting for a fairly high, dry site, while she and Callie sat on the shaky dock and watched the water swirl and foam around the debris coming downstream. "I think we got a little of Noah's flood," she said, when Joseph returned with a triumphant look on his face. "Let's just hope we can stay above it."

"I found us a good place, Miz Judy," he said, helping her lead the mounts toward a stand of pine trees some distance inland.

He was right. The low mound was topped with a thick

mat of pine needles, and the trees formed almost a roof above it. She wondered, as she shook out bedding and helped tie up the tarp, that a natural hillock should be so regularly shaped, as if some giant had turned a pudding basin upside down there.

When David came up from the river, he was nodding. "We'll get a ride across tomorrow. Gaines has been on the other side for a week, trapped because the water was too high to risk. Now it's going down, and Jock, back there, knows his boss will get here as soon as he can. We need a good night's sleep anyway."

They rested well, despite a chorus of frogs croaking in every conceivable tone and rhythm and a mockingbird in the tree above their shelter that went through its entire repertory a dozen times. Judith was too weary to hear or care. When she opened her eyes, the sky was pink, and she knew the sun might shine today. Perhaps the river would go down enough to allow a crossing.

BORN REBEL

CONCLUSION

Here my story ended, but here also is a summary of what I intended:

Once across the Sabine River, David and Judith find themselves in thickly grown forest filled with mosquitoes and snakes. The going is very rough, and when they arrive at a cabin that offers shelter and food, David arranges for them to rest there for several days at the Wyler residence. Unfortunately, when he pays for their accommodations, someone in the family glimpses gold.

When the McCarrans leave, their erstwhile hosts' two grown sons follow, intending to kill them in the forest and take whatever they have. Fortunately, David and Judith are still watchful, keeping their arms ready for any attack, and they manage to take out the two Wyler sons who come after them.

As they move on westward, Jonas Bluth arrives and manages to get passage across the river. The Wylers are furious at the disappearance of their boys, and Jonas promises to wreak vengeance on the McCarrans when he catches up with them.

When he does, he finds a terrible surprise waiting for him, as Judith, armed and weary of constant worry, shoots him dead as he crawls into their camp by night.

Once in Nacogdoches, the administrative center of the

area, David arranges for a land grant, 600 acres, and he and his family begin building and cultivating. However, the local alcalde becomes so demanding that the McCarrans relinquish their claim and buy a farm from a widow who is unable to work her remote acreage.

There they build a new life for themselves, their growing family, and for Joseph and his family, whom they decide to free from slavery and to give a share of the land and the livestock. When David dies of snakebite, Judith continues to work the farm, with the help of her black partners and her children.

THE GUNS OF LIVINGSTON FROST:

A WASHINGTON SHIPP MYSTERY

This would have been the third novel in a series featuring Washington Shipp, the black Police Chief and later Sheriff of the county. Death in the Square *and* Body in the Swamp *are the two preceding novels in this series. I wish I had been able to complete this one as well.*

THE GUNS OF LIVINGSTON FROST

CHAPTER ONE

WASHINGTON SHIPP

Amy, his secretary, had stacked the morning's Texas and out-of-state reports neatly on Wash's desk, to wait for him to finish reading through the overnight reports from his own deputies. Since running for sheriff and winning, he had learned a new set of duties, for some of which his time as Police Chief of Templeton, Texas, had not prepared him. Before, he had not felt a need to keep up with crimes taking place very far outside of his own jurisdiction. Now he shuddered and picked up the pile of printouts, which he scanned through quickly. Some were too distant to concern him, he felt sure, but he found among the sheets one that made him pause.

Some knowledgeable burglar in the Arkansas-Texas-Louisiana region was stealing antique firearms, very selectively. This was the fourth incident of the kind that he had seen cross his desk, and Wash felt sure that this was a sort of steal-to-order ring, fencing to some dealer with nationwide or international connections.

While some might have thought Templeton too remote and unsophisticated to offer much scope for the attentions of such a group, Washington Shipp knew better. He had known the Frost family since he was a small black boy, growing up in the river bottoms beyond their family home on the outskirts of town.

Livingston Frost, the grandson of his grandfather's one-time employer, was presently one of the foremost dealers in antique firearms in the entire country. His stock, which Wash had examined back when he was Police Chief, was amazing. He had added to his own family's collection by trading, buying, and selling, until it was almost unequaled.

If this gang was as well informed as it seemed to be, from reading the list of victims and stolen items, one day it was going to target the guns of Livingston Frost. Wash reached for his telephone and punched in the familiar number. The phone rang several times before a hesitant voice said, "Hello?"

"Miss Frost, is your brother at home? This is Sheriff Shipp, and I really do need to speak to him, if possible." The timid voice grew a bit stronger.

"Oh, Wash! I was afraid it might be...some stranger. No, Stony is away at a gun show. He won't be home until the end of the week, he said when he called last night."

Wash sighed. He certainly couldn't alarm poor Lily, who had problems of her own, with this rather nebulous concern he felt. The best he could do was to ask her to have her brother call him when he returned. A nebulous hunch wasn't enough to justify getting his number at his hotel and calling him at the show.

After he hung up the phone, he sat for a moment, wondering about the woman who waited alone in the old family home. Always shy and insecure, she was now a recluse. Yet Lily, of all people, had engaged in a wild and adventurous escapade that few recalled now. She had been gone from Templeton for almost two years, and when she returned she was damaged both mentally and physically. Wash still wondered about that, though he had not asked any questions. He and Stony were friends, but not as close as all that.

Yet Washington Shipp felt a closeness to that family, as he did to all those under his care. Other sheriffs might have been corrupt or unwise or uncaring, but he had determined, when he ran for office, to be the caretaker of his county. Now he felt a small shiver of apprehension, but he shook it away. He could not allow his hunches to control his work.

Then the phone rang, and the sheriff returned to his job, forgetting his concerns in the complex problems that even a relatively small county seemed to generate constantly.

THE GUNS OF LIVINGSTON FROST

CHAPTER TWO

LIVINGSTON FROST

It was raining. That wasn't unusual in East Texas in the winter, but Livingston Frost hated dampness and chill. His warped body ached worse in such weather. That, he thought, was what made him feel so apprehensive and ill-at-ease as he drove into his garage.

The weather set his bones to twinging, sending stabs of agony through his small frame. The polio that withered his left leg and twisted his back when he was nine years old had left a legacy of pain that had been his constant companion for most of his forty-odd years.

He leaned heavily on his cane, as he hurried from the garage toward the big dark house, whose dour face reminded him of the Scots grandfather who had built it: it looked disapproving. In the rain it all but scowled at anyone bold enough to venture into its curving porch. But now he had no time for whimsy, even though he leavened his limited and joyless life with such wry humor.

Lily would have the coffeepot on and a supper of soup and salad and homemade bread waiting. He had been gone for a week, this time, attending a particularly promising showing of antique firearms, which led to a visit to the home of an important customer.

She always missed him dreadfully. He was to his sister

what she was to him, the sole companion of a lonely life. He never allowed himself to wonder what would happen to her if he should die. Their only relative was very elderly, unlikely to survive for long.

His key turned in the stiff lock, and the door moved open, the hall breathing into his face its usual smell of furniture polish and mildew. But there was something else— something subtly wrong with the feel of the house. His illness had left Frost painfully aware of atmosphere, and tonight his home was filled with something forbidding.

"Lily! Are you here?" he called. The place was entirely too still. She should have been in the hall as soon as his feet thumped unevenly across the porch, her gawky shape hurrying to greet him, her long braid flapping behind her. She endured his business trips with impatience tinged with misery.

There was no answer from the depths of the house. The twilight outside did nothing to lessen the darkness within, and he touched the switch for the lamps. Nothing happened. Had the storm caused a power outage? He had noticed the street lamps were burning in the early darkness outside. Whatever the problem was, it had to be the house's own system.

Grumbling a bit, he fumbled blindly in the drawer of the breakfront beside the parlor door and found a candle. Matches waited beside it, and he struck a light and looked about.

It seemed the storm must have gone through the interior of the house. Furniture was overturned or pushed out of place, though the mahogany Victorian pieces were too heavy to damage much. A ruby glass vase that had been his grandmother's lay shattered on the Persian carpet, blood-colored shards picking up the faint glimmers from his candle. Frost's heart thumped uncomfortably in his throat. His sister was his only close companion. Even with her mental problems, left over from her brief flirtation with LSD, she kept his house clean and comfortable.

Her infrequent lapses into delusion were a small price to pay for her company. While he had never thought to wonder if he loved her, he knew that he needed her, even as she did him, to help give him some semblance of normal life.

"Lily?" he croaked again, holding his stick now as a weapon, instead of a prop.

He moved into the hall leading to the dining room and the kitchen. There was no sound from upstairs or down. Listening intently, he went along haltingly, trying to see into the many rooms along the crowded corridor. The candle's frail flame did little to help his search.

Now his stomach had curled into a tight knot, and the hand holding the candle was shaking. He had always been frail, without physical strength. Now he wondered if he might be a coward as well. He dreaded going into the kitchen at the end of the corridor; it took all his will-power to push open the swinging door. For a moment, he thought the room was empty of anyone. There was little that could be disturbed there. He had modernized the place with built-ins, for the convenience of his sister, once his business had become really profitable.

As he stared about, he could see a drift of flour over the floor. The trail led into a shadow beyond the marble-topped work table that Lily had insisted upon keeping for making pastry and kneading bread. She lay there, a cracked bowl by her hand and the flour sifter on its side beyond her. There was blood on her forehead.

He went down onto one knee, awkward and unsure about his ability to cope with this calamity. "Lily, oh, Lily," he mourned, lifting her head into a more comfortable position and trying to wipe away the drying blood with his immaculate handkerchief.

She sighed and groaned, and something inside him relaxed a bit. She was alive. He had not been left entirely alone in the dark confines of their home, to be comforted only by the chilly presence of his antique weapons. And that thought brought him up short.

The house did not promise wealth by its appearance. It looked, instead, like a place filled with the preserved aura of Victorianism, as it was, preserving the long family traditions and most of its possessions. Only his guns were valuable—and they were extremely valuable, though most of those in the house were renovated ones that he used for display. His most valuable stock was kept in the vault at the Templeton Bank. This break-in might have been made to look like the work of vandals, but he wondered why random kids would pick such a secluded neighborhood and such an unpromising house for their activities. Seldom, he understood, did the rascals choose to violate a home where someone was present.

On the other hand, professional thieves after his rather famous firearms collection might try to make this look like pointless violence. It would make a certain amount of sense.

Lily groaned. "Martin?" she murmured, her voice thick and unfamiliar. "Don't hit me again, Martin!"

Frost gritted his teeth. That name had not passed her lips in twenty years, since the day she appeared on the steps of this house, all her possessions in a knapsack on her back. It was instinct—the inbuilt ability to find home again—that had brought her through the fog of drugs, out of her unstable, hippy-style existence, and back into the family home and his life.

Then, too, she had been bruised and bloody. If he had been able to find Martin Fewell, he would have shot him, being quite incapable of doing anything more actively physical, like beating the brute to a pulp.

She opened her eyes, staring up from the hazed depths of her confusion "Stony? It's you? They came to the door. They kicked it in. Stony, they took your guns!"

Frost helped her to sit up, fury building inside him until he was afraid his fragile body couldn't hold it. "Who were they?" he asked.

She might not be able to come up with a clear and usable description. She was sharp, now that her past had receded, but she had periods of being spaced out and incoherent, usually following an emotional upset. She seemed to be pulling her thoughts together as she sat for a moment, then stood, with some difficulty.

She was taller than he, heavier, and uncrippled. She helped him up, rather than the reverse, but she did it absently, her gaze seeming to be fixed on some point out of the normal range. Frost tugged at her elbow and got her into the rocking chair that their mother had insisted on keeping in her kitchen, long past the days when she rocked her infants in it.

"You sit here, and I'll make coffee—or maybe tea would be better for you. Who was it, Lily? Can you identify them?" He took the kettle from beneath the sink.

"They got your guns. The ones on the wall in the den. The ones in the glass case in the living room. I couldn't get up, but I saw them come back with them. Will this ruin us, Stony?" Her eyes were foggy, still, but he thought she seemed to be gaining control.

"I keep the most valuable guns in the vault at the bank," he reminded her.

She nodded slowly, but he thought she wasn't really hearing what he said. "The big one was mean," she murmured. "Just like Martin, with a black beard like his. I bit him on the arm."

Frost looked down at her in surprise. In all the time she had lived with Martin, she had never stood up to him, she'd told him. Had something in their quiet life together finally given her the backbone to fight back?

"And how many were there?" he asked, afraid he might distract her from her unstable concentration.

"Four. Two were little blond fellows, just alike. But one had a scar on his hand. I saw it when he hit me. It looked like a W, across the back of his right hand. The other one didn't come close enough for me to see. He was just a big man in a raincoat and a wide hat." She closed her eyes and sighed deeply, as the cut over her eye began to ooze blood again.

Frost filled the teakettle. Then he wet his handkerchief. As he dabbed at the cut, he thought furiously. She was lucid. That was wonderful. She could describe these villains, and she might even be able to testify, if the police ever caught them. Lily was definitely getting better. She held the wet cloth to her head, as he dialed the sheriff's department. But the phone was dead—they must have cut the wires before breaking into the house, probably when they pulled the circuit breaker.

"You sit still," he told his sister. "I'm going to drive to the corner and call Wash Shipp."

She stared at him as if trying to recall something. Then she said, "He called you, the other day. Said for you to get in touch...but he didn't say why...." Her voice trailed off.

Again he went through the rain into a darkness studded by dazzling droplets lit by the street lamps, to reach the car. Even furious and worried as he was, he wondered if this shock and her ability to resist might be the very thing Lily had needed to bring her out of her twenty-year-long daze. And yet he had a bad feeling about the entire matter. Those were dangerous men, he felt. Too dangerous to meddle with.

He backed into the empty street and headed toward the convenience store, chewing at his lower lip. He had marked those relatively valueless rebuilt guns he displayed in the house, etching his Social Security number in hidden places. He could identify all of them or any part of them, from barrel to grip strap.

If, by some fluke, the police caught the men with their

loot, he could nail them. If Lily could stand up to a trial, she could identify three of them. He intended to hang the bastards out to dry, no matter what it took to accomplish it.

The phone rang, and he steadied his voice, which tended to be shaky. "Amy?" he asked. When she replied, "No, it's Lucy," he said, "I need to report something really serious.

THE GUNS OF LIVINGSTON FROST

CHAPTER THREE

WASHINGTON SHIPP

Washington Shipp was not a patient man, and he disliked criminals with all his might. He despised sneak thieves and vandals, of course, and he dealt with any who were caught operating in his bailiwick as sternly as the law allowed. He detested burglars, and anyone who attacked one of the people in his charge turned up his emotional thermostat to the boiling point.

He had hoped, on this rainy evening, to go home and watch TV with his nine-year-old son, while his wife worked on her weekly column for the *Templeton Signal*. The call from Livingston Frost put the kibosh on that.

"Break-in at 6411 Oak Grove Lane," the dispatcher said, as she came out of her office. "That Frost fellow who deals in antique guns. Might be a big haul there if they got any of his choice pieces. I went to his gun show last year, and there was stuff there that would make you drool."

Nobody would have picked dumpy little Lucy Fowler as an antique weapons enthusiast, he reflected. "I'd like to get rid of every last gun in the world," Shipp growled. "What does he report missing?"

"He didn't say anything about missing property. He was boiling over because the men who broke into the house hurt his sister. You know, Lily, who went off to be a hippy and came back with her wits addled."

"Badly?" The question came so fast and so sharply that Mrs. Fowler blinked.

"Hit her on the head, he told me. I've sent Sterling and Lambert to check things out. That okay? They were patrolling only about a half a mile away." She was watching him, reading him, he knew. She'd known him since he was a teenager doing chores for the wealthy families in town, and it sometimes made him uncomfortable to think how closely she could predict what he'd do.

"Lucy, you know I'm going out there, don't you? My granddaddy worked for Dr. Frost and I've always known Stony and Lily. No matter what mistakes she made when she was young and foolish, she's a friend. I want to see with my own eyes what happened."

She grinned, the rouge on her faintly wrinkled cheeks crinkling into pink relief. "I've already told 'em you would be there. Jim has your car out front, waiting for you."

He half chuckled, as he pulled on his leather jacket. It was sometimes very handy to have your needs met before you knew you needed them, but he would have liked, just once, to surprise that woman! He had a feeling that would never happen, though, for she could predict things she knew nothing about and could not explain at all. It was some kind of gift, he supposed.

The roads were slick with rain, and reflections of on-coming lights, brightly lit signs, and street lamps glimmered on the black mirror of the asphalt. He squinted, trying to separate the real from the illusory. He was using his eyes too hard these days, with the interminable reports he had to read and write. But it grew much darker as he got out into the remote area where Frost lived.

Oak Grove Lane had been a county road ten years ago. Only fishermen going to the river with their boats and gear had used it, or farmers bringing in produce from their low-lying farms. Woods still grew along most of its length, broken only by old homes like the Frost house or by a few new brick mansions, each surrounded by its own acreage of trees and grass.

The Frosts had owned a thousand acres, once upon a time, reaching all the way down to the Nichayac River. It was only by selling off bits of land that young Livingston had managed to keep things together after his father died. The Frosts were what the local people called land-poor— lots of land, no money.

Strangely enough, it had been Lucy Fowler who had led young Frost into what became his business. She had known his father well; indeed, everyone in the county had known old Doctor Frost and most had come into the world under his gentle touch. She had shared the old man's interest in antique weapons, even before the collecting craze hit its peak in the Seventies.

When she pointed out to Livingston that his father's and grandfather's collections were worth a great deal of money, that had set him on the road to financial independence. Now his trading, buying, and selling were a part of the intricate network of antique firearms collecting in America, and had become, Wash knew, a highly profitable business.

And that, once he thought about it, scared the sheriff. He had already had the notion that there might be "special order" thieves who knew where anything could be found, and who took orders and delivered the goods as dependably as Sears, Roebuck ever had. The difference was that their stock was stolen to order.

The road curved to miss a huge maple that leaned over the way. The Frost driveway looped to the left, just past the tree, and a dim glow shone through the dripping privet and holly to guide him into the parking area before the garage. A police car was pulled off to one side, and Frost's own modest Toyota was halfway inside the shelter.

Shipp slammed his door and strode through the wet into the haven of the porch. The many-bulbed lamp had been lit, though the total wattage came to something like fifty, he decided. The door opened before he could knock, and young Lambert nodded as he stepped back to let him enter.

"Lucy said you were coming, Sheriff. They made a mess of the place, broke some antique glass, scratched up the furniture a bit. We were able to find the circuit box and get the power back on, which helps. The lady isn't hurt much, but Mr. Frost's display guns were all taken."

Wash's scowl reflected his feelings on that score. Not that he thought that antique weapons were going to be used by criminals—there were more efficient weapons to be stolen far more easily. But the idea gave him the cold robbies.

He followed Lambert down the dark hallway toward the kitchen, where the smell of coffee was beginning to warm the air. Lily was sitting in a Lincoln rocker, sipping a cup of tea, and Frost was perched on a tall stool, his thin face paper-white, his black hair curled from the damp.

He stood as the sheriff entered. "Wash! Glad you came. I've been trying to persuade Lily that what was stolen isn't my real stock, just my rebuilt models for show, so to speak. Maybe you can make her accept that. She always liked you."

Shipp took the offered kitchen chair and turned it to straddle the seat. "As I don't know myself, you tell me, and we'll see if this time around it will take."

"Oh." Frost seemed at a loss for a moment. Then he climbed back onto his stool and ran a slender hand through his hair.

"Well, to begin with, I keep all my valuable stock in a vault in the bank. My dad did before me, and even Grand-dad began storing his best pieces there when they built the storage facility for large valuables, though the real collecting fever hadn't begun yet to power the trade in stolen antiques.

"So what you could see on my walls and in my cabinets here were either replicas, which aren't worth much, or rebuilt weapons that had deteriorated so much I had to replace too many parts to allow them to be sold as really good antique specimens. You following that?"

Shipp nodded. "Sounds logical to me. You could show them to your customers to give an idea what you had, and then if they were interested, you'd get the real thing out and sell it to them."

"Right. But still the pieces here weren't worthless. They were valued at about three thousand dollars in all for my insurance policy. That isn't much per piece, but it is enough to make this grand larceny, isn't it? I want to nail those bastards with everything I can. They hit Lily!"

Wash, despite himself, had always had a certain innate contempt for weakness, no matter what its cause. Now he regarded Frost with a new respect. The fellow couldn't help being crippled. And now he was mad as a wet wasp, ready to go to war, it seemed.

"We're going to get them," he said. He turned to Lily. "You tell me what they looked like, Lily-bird."

She looked up for the first time, the old nickname rousing her as nothing else had done since he arrived. "Washington? You're here? That's nice...." She drifted away again.

Frost left his stool to kneel beside the rocker, his withered leg making a hard job of it. "Lily, honey, tell us what they looked like. Okay?"

She stared down at him, up at the sheriff. "All right," she sighed. "One was big and had a dark beard. He looked quite a bit like Martin. Martin...Fewell."

That told Wash a great deal, for he had taken an instant dislike to Martin Fewell when they both were boys, and that grew worse the day he got drunk, came to town and picked a fight in the drugstore. When Lily left town with the fellow, he had known she was making a bad mistake. He knew what Martin looked like. Yes, indeed.

"Then there were two small men, both blond. Twins. They had narrow little faces like foxes, and one had a scar—you tell him about it later, Stony. I'm tired."

"Three then—that was all you saw?"

"No. There was another one, but he was wrapped up in a raincoat, with a big wide hat, and I couldn't see his face. He didn't come close to me at all."

She seemed drained, and the trail of dried blood down her cheek, beneath the bandage, made her look like the survivor of some disaster. Which, in a way, she was.

"Lily, can you tell me, for certain, that these were the men, if I call you to testify? If we catch them?" He watched her face closely, as she considered.

"S-sometimes I'm scared. I go and hide in my room for days. But I'll try. I'll try."

He looked up at Frost. "I think that's enough. Come talk to me, Stony. We can let your sister rest now."

He, too, was boiling. Any thief who thought he could come into Washington Shipp's county and break into houses and hit lone women was going to find that life was very uncomfortable from that time forward.

He got everything Frost could provide. Then he went around the house, inside and out, while the fingerprint man did his job. They got a couple of dabs that were neither those of Lily nor of Livingston. They found those on the circuit box, which was hard to open with gloves on.

By the time everything was in hand, he had a good idea of his next step. He sent out a region-wide bulletin, using the descriptions he had, and he sent the fingerprints to the FBI, along with the identifying numbers and features of all the stolen guns. He had a feeling the men were already out of the area, but he also had a gut instinct that they might well be back, sooner or later. Particularly when they found out that the guns they had stolen were relatively worthless. They might well try again.

THE GUNS OF LIVINGSTON FROST

CHAPTER FOUR

MYRON DUSON

The black van went streaking down the highway, tearing a bright trail of light through the seamless darkness of the countryside. The state highway was busy in the daytime, but at night few vehicles used it, and tiny hamlets provided the only swift points of brightness in the long stretches of forest and pastureland that lined the way.

Myron Duson knew just about every inch of back road in all of East Texas and the western half of Louisiana. He planned his jobs carefully, and he never left any loose ends, which was why he was feeling antsy now.

"You sure that bitch was dead?" he asked for the third time in the past five miles. "She kept staring at me like she knew me. Made me mighty nervous. She'd know me again, Crowley. Didn't seem to me you hit her hard enough."

David Crowley didn't turn his head as he replied, "Myron, you're gettin' old and scary. 'Course she's dead. I hit her a lick, I tell you. Besides, we're clean out of that country now, and we'll be in Shreveport before you can say scat. Our client is going to go ape over these guns we got." The dim light from the dash showed the small man's profile and a straggle of pale hair.

Myron sighed and looked back at the road. Something had gone sour, and he wasn't able to put his finger on just what it might be.

"You got the scanner hooked up yet?" he asked over his shoulder.

Donald Crowley grunted, behind him. Then he said, "Here. It's hooked into the power supply—listen good, Myron. You're gettin' all shook for nothin'." There came a click, and the hum of the scanner was broken by a distant chatter of talk. "...try findin' a naked nigger on a dark night for yourself!" came through plaintively in a thick redneck accent, and all the men in the van snickered.

A stronger signal brought a string of directions and code numbers. Then: "All Points Bulletin. Repeat All Points Bulletin. Wanted for assault and burglary of a dwelling, four men, probably traveling together.

"Male Caucasian, five feet, eleven inches, about a hundred eighty pounds, dark hair and beard, black eyes, dark complexion. Two male Caucasians, twins, blond, narrow faces, scar on back of right hand of one shaped like a W. One male, probably Caucasian or Scandinavian but uncertain, large, heavy, dark raincoat, black hat with wide brim."

"By God, I told you that you didn' hit her hard enough!" Duson shouted over the rumble of the engine. "She's alive, and Frost got back and found her. Now we're goin' to have every highway patrol all over the area looking for anything suspicious." He slowed to the speed limit, and the noise of the engine quieted a bit.

"Myron, if her head is that hard, you couldn't have dented it yourself," David snapped. "Here, turn right up at the next crossroad. There's a dirt road I know that will take us over to Highway 21. That'll get us over the line, and from there it's just a hop, skip, and a jump to Shreveport. We can circle off to the east and hit our man's driveway without going onto any main road."

The van slowed still more, and within a half hour it was bumping along over the ruts of a muddy country lane. Sure enough, in a couple of hours it ended at the narrow pavement of 21, and they turned with great relief toward the Louisiana line.

Myron was not happy, but things seemed to be straightening themselves out at last. They hit 171 to Shreveport by midnight, and there was no talk of a bulletin out on them, once they crossed into the next state. Things were going to be all right, and this special order would be delivered on time and in fine fashion. The broker should pay a good price for the pieces in the back of the van.

He snorted and shifted his position. What anybody would want with a bunch of ancient guns that probably would blow up in your face if you tried to fire them he didn't know. The polished stocks, the elaborate engravings on barrels and plates, the loving care with which they had been made and used didn't touch him. A good sound Uzi, now, could make tears come to his eyes. This stuff was a bunch of crap.

They bypassed Shreveport, approaching their goal from the southeast. Bollivar's drive was hard to find in the dark—or the daylight, for that matter—but he hit it unerringly, and the van pulled out of sight among the overhanging crepe myrtles and mimosas, behind the trimmed privet hedges.

As soon as the engine died, a light came on in the big garage into which they had pulled. The doors went down silently, hiding the transaction that was to take place, even if the only witness might be the damp greenery. Myron opened his door and got out, his knees stiff with the damp and with sitting for so long.

"Easy haul?" asked a voice, and a thin fellow wearing a velvet jacket came into the light from a door connecting the garage with the house beside it.

"Not so you'd notice," said Myron. He unlocked the

rear doors of the van and pulled them wide. "There was a damned woman there—nobody tol' me Frost lived with somebody. We walked right in and there she was in the kitchen. Couldn' see any light from outside at all. Made it sticky, I tell you."

The man stiffened, his pale eyes narrowing. "And...?" he asked.

"Dave hit her. Not hard enough. There was a bulletin out, back in Texas. Probably not here. At least, not yet." Myron was disgusted, and his voice reflected that.

Bollivar relaxed a bit. "Might as well check out the goods," he said, moving to peer into the darkness inside the van. "You, Septien, hand me whatever's on top."

A dark-skinned hand came into view, holding an oddly shaped gun wrapped in plastic. Bollivar slipped the plastic off and eyed the piece. His eyes lit up, but Myron knew that it was with greed, not with the collector's true fanaticism.

"This looks like a Wesson sport rifle. Short barrel. It's in really fine condition—I think I can get a good price for it. If the rest come up to this one, you're going to be able to take off for a while and let things cool down."

The other twin had crawled out the front, and now the last man came sliding out the rear of the van. "Don' you fool yourself," he said. His yellow-brown eyes were filled with wicked amusement in the stark light of the garage.

"I been looking, back there, wit' my little flash. These is all real, yes and true, but they not what you want, Meester Bollivar. These is for show, they not for sale. Not to collector, you bet." He chuckled, his swarthy face wrinkled into a mask.

"What would you know about what collectors want?" the broker asked, his mouth tight.

"Old Maurice, he be in the business for a long time, man. I work wid him when I be a boy. Maurice, he know a hawk from a handsaw any day of the week. He know jewel, he know gun, he know old furniture, he know everything anybody want, any time, any place. An' he teach me.

"You look at those gun. Every piece be mark; you look. That Fros' man, he too smart to risk his business in that old rattletrap house that anybody get in with two hairpin and a strong breath of air."

Bollivar was frowning, and Myron felt as if he might burst, himself. The Crowleys stood off to one side, their heads cocked in opposite directions, as if they were mirror images. Their identical faces held no expression.

The broker's fingers moved surely, and the stock came off the Wesson. He peered into the depths of the piece, and his frown became ferocious.

When he looked up, Myron dreaded the message in his eyes. "You've got a load of trash," he said. "Marked trash, too. Why didn't you check to see where he kept the good stuff? You've wasted your time and my time, and you've got your heads in a noose in Texas.

"You idiots! I don't know why I waste my talents working with the likes of you! I'll have to get Simpson's bunch to fill the order, I suppose. And who else has such a lovely stock, just what the client wants?" He sighed and stalked from the bright garage.

The light went off and the door went up.

Myron cleared his throat. "Get the Wesson back in the van. We'll dump this lot in the first likely spot we see. Then we're goin' back and get rid of that woman. She's the only one can put us in Dutch, and we've got to get rid of her, permanent."

* * * * * * *

The night was still dark and wet, but there was little traffic, and they made good time as they picked up Highway 171 again. "We'll go down past De Ridder and turn back east on 196," David said, studying the shining ribbon of road ahead of them.

"That will put us back close, without having to travel far through Texas. Nobody will expect us to be heading back toward Templeton, anyway. We can get there in time to hide out until it's dark again. Then we can slip up and see what goes on at that house. I'll bet that woman is there by herself again." His eyes gleamed, and he glanced down at the bite-mark on Duson's arm.

Myron growled deep in his throat and picked up speed. He had good reason to want to put that woman down.

They went through Many very early in the morning. Few cars were on the streets, and Myron took care to drive exactly at the speed limit, yet a cop-car turned a corner behind them and hit its lights. The siren wailed them to a stop.

The policeman looked sleepy and out of sorts. When Myron handed out his driver's license, the officer shone a flashlight back into the body of the van. That woke him completely.

Duson saw the hand go for the gun, and he rolled over the engine housing, over Crowley's lap, and out the far door before the officer could fire. They were alongside a closed service station, whose apron disappeared behind it into darkness broken by the shapes of trees. Myron dashed for that cover, hearing a single set of footsteps following him. He pushed through a screen of bushes, and the footing went out from under him, letting him drop into dark space. He hit with a splash in knee-deep water, cold as a witch's tit, and another splash told him that one of his men had made it with him.

"Who?" he breathed.

"Septien," came the reply. "We move fas', my frien'. That cop, he call for backup. They be here any minute, an' we better be gone. I don' know thees place. They do. We cross, you theenk?"

ARDATH MAYHAR * 103

Myron pushed up the muddy bank on the far side of the creek. There was a thick stand of pines there, and he went deep into it before it began to thin again, letting onto a quiet residential street. Cars were parked in the semi-darkness between the light standards, and nothing moved except a prowling cat, which whisked across the street and into the shelter of an old fashioned veranda.

"You give me one minute," came Septien's quiet voice, "an' I have one of these theeng go."

He was as good as his word. Without a sound, the Cajun opened the door of a pale gray Mazda and slid under the steering wheel. A few deft motions of his fingers brought a cough, and the engine fired, quietly enough not to wake the sleepers in the nearby houses.

Myron piled into the other side, and they crept away from the curb without turning on the lights. At the corner, Septien pulled the switch, and twin beams glared into the early morning dimness. They stopped at the stop-sign.

Three police cars were pulled up alongside the main street-*cum*-highway, and the van was surrounded by a swarm of uniformed men. Myron cursed softly, as the twins were dragged out of the rear doors and bundled unceremoniously into a vehicle.

That didn't do a thing to make him any happier. He had done a job that turned sour. He had lost the van and half his force. He had a grudge, and when Myron Duson was angry, it was time to go home and lock all the doors.

THE GUNS OF LIVINGSTON FROST

CHAPTER FIVE

LILY FROST

Lily lay flat on her back in the four-poster in which her grandmother had given birth to eight stillborn children, one daughter, and her father. She had died there, too, at the age of seventy-one, but that didn't trouble her granddaughter. Dying was the only thing in her existence that she had never felt frightened about.

Many other things terrified her, however, the worst being Martin. Sometimes she had nightmares in which he came bursting into the house, struck down Stony, and dragged her away again into the abusive, drug-ridden life she had escaped.

When those men had broken the door and confronted her, she had been certain that they were led by her former lover and worst enemy. It had been desperation, she was sure, that gave her the courage to bite the man who grabbed her, setting her teeth into his hairy arm until she tasted blood. She hoped he got tetanus from that bite—or hydrophobia!

She turned restlessly, twisting the blanket and the hand made quilt so that she had to straighten them out again. Then she stared at the dim glimmer of light from the yard lamp outside, which was reflected in the mirror.

It looked as wet as the stormy night. The flap of drenched branches against the wooden siding kept making her jump, her nerves jolting every time.

There was a light tap at the door, and she smiled faintly. That would be Stony, worried about her.

"Yes," she murmured, and the door opened to admit his slight shape.

He was carrying a teacup, which he balanced with great care, for his limp tended to slosh liquids. "Here, I thought you might need this. I've got some sleeping stuff, too, that the doctor gave me. Do you want that, too?"

She sat and pushed back the covers, swinging her long legs over the edge of the bed and reaching for her robe. "No. Thanks, Stony. Just the tea. That should relax me and let me sleep. You know I don't take anything, now. Not anything at all. Something might react with the LSD and set things off again, here when I'm just now getting on top of the flashbacks."

He nodded, as he backed to sit in her small rocker. The fitful light, finding its way through swaying branches to her window, danced on his face, which seemed thinner and paler than ever after the evening's events. He looked entirely too frail, she realized, and the thought frightened her.

For once, her concern was greater than her internal terrors. "Stony," she said, reaching for the cup he had set on the dressing table, "you need to take something yourself. You look like a ghost. I will be all right—I always am." She shivered as she sipped the hot tea, into which he had put a dollop of Grandfather's brandy.

"Lily, we've got to talk. I wasn't able, before, but you ought to know what's going to happen. If they put you on the witness stand, when they catch those men, whoever defends them is going to tear you apart, trying to make it seem you aren't a reliable witness. Have you thought about that?" He leaned forward, his hands tight on the curved arms of the rocker.

She sank onto the edge of the bed, warming her hands around the cup. She could see herself in the mirror, a dim ghost of a reflection with huge eyes that were wells of shadow. More like me than I am in the daylight, she thought. She turned back to her brother. "I know. I've...been on a witness stand before. I never told you, because I hate to remember it. That one did it, too. He made me look like a crazy, dope-ridden woman who couldn't understand what was going on, no matter what she thought she saw. And the jury believed it.

"That's why..."—she took a long draught of the tea, warming herself to the pit of her stomach against the memory—"...that's why I ran away and came home.

"They let Martin out, you see, and he knew I'd testified against him. He killed...but you don't want to know about that. I don't want to remember it. He came after me, and I ran. I've been expecting him ever since." She gave a long shuddering sigh.

"When I thought those men were Martin, I knew there was no reason for being afraid any more. They were going to kill me, and if I could make them sorry I was going to do it. I wish—I wish I had done the same thing to Martin, a long time before he killed that kid. Things might have been different, if I had."

Stony was staring at her, his eyes wide and his face tense. "I didn't know, dear. It isn't going to be easy, but we'll be in it together. You are dead certain you can identify—but of course you are. I'll go away and let you sleep, now." He rose stiffly and limped away down the hall, leaving her staring, once again, at the ceiling.

This time, she was relaxed. The hot tea and the brandy had loosed her muscles and her mind, and she knew she could sleep now.

But instead she chose to relive that old trial, which she had thought forever lost in the fogs of the past....

* * * * * *

"You saw this man, Martin Fewell, attack Samuel Bar-
rett? With your own eyes? You were present at the struggle?" The defense counsel's hard gray eyes bored into
hers, making her throat constrict.

"I was there, yes. And I saw Martin hit him with his
fists. Then, when the boy got up again, he picked up a two-
by-four and hit him over the head with it. He beat his head
until the board sounded squashy when it hit." There, it
was out, and she hadn't faltered.

"But had you not taken drugs during the evening?
Mind-altering drugs, which often produce delusions in the
minds of those who take them? Lysergic acid diethylamide,
to be exact, or LSD?" His gaze was intent, intimidating.

"Martin gave me things, yes, but not that day. I had
nothing that day, and I know what I saw. I saw Martin kill
Sammy." She felt tears starting in her eyes, and she felt,
also, Martin's glare from his seat at the defense table.

The lawyer leaned forward like a wolf about to kill.
"But is it not true that you sometimes have what is known
as flashbacks, sudden episodes of disorientation caused by
the drug, even when you have had none for some time?"

It was true. She nodded, wordless, and bent her head
to stare into her lap. But that wasn't what happened! She
cried inside herself. She knew it was hopeless...Martin was
about to get away with murder.

* * * * * *

Lily sighed softly. She had lived through that and
through Martin's search for her afterward. She would survive this, too. She closed her eyes and slept.

But among her restless dreams, a dim shape prowled,
sometimes as Martin, sometimes as that other man who
resembled him so closely. She sat again in that courtroom,

but this time it was Stony whose death she remembered, and it was that other Martin who had killed him.

She forced herself out of the depths of her dream and sat, her eyes wide, staring at the shadow of the branches on the wall. Fury built inside her, burning away at the residue of timidity that had troubled her for so long.

"Nobody is going to hurt my brother!" she whispered, clenching her long fingers into fists. "I will not let anyone hurt Stony!"

Somehow, that resolve eased her inner tensions. When she slept again, it was dreamlessly and well.

THE GUNS OF LIVINGSTON FROST

CHAPTER SIX

LIVINGSTON FROST

The next morning was a difficult one for Livingston. He had been so sick with worry about his sister, the night before, that he had given no thought to what had happened to his home. But now, in the newly washed sunlight, he could see the traces where those men had passed. He felt as if dirty hands had touched him.

The furniture, while some was scratched, was undamaged, testifying to the staying power of solid Philippine mahogany. The ruby glass was unrepairable, and Lily vacuumed the spot where it had smashed, after they picked up the curving shards with careful fingers.

It took some time to get the house into order again, but even then it felt as if a secure stronghold had been breached. It would never be the same again. The places on the walls where his showpieces had hung reminded him, when he looked up, that he had lost pieces that he was fond of, though they were not really valuable.

The Baby Dragoon Revolver that had been his grandfather's was one that he wished, now, he had put into the bank. It had had extensive repair, but the old man carried it for years, and it was one he wanted to keep. Now it was in the hands of thieves—he shook the thought away and turned to stare around the big parlor.

"It feels as if somebody has ruined something important," he mused.

Lily straightened and stared into his face, her eyes wide. "Yes. That's the way Martin made me feel, all the time. I thought I was through with that, and here it comes again.

"Last night—Stony, I was scared out of my wits, last night. But somehow I came through it. Out the other side, you know? After you left, I got hold of myself. I think things will be all right now."

She was a bit pale, the bandage on her head making her look rather jaunty. She was polishing the big claw-footed table in the center of the room, rubbing with lemon oil as if to remove the taint of those who had violated their space. Something was troubling her, he could tell, but he waited until she was ready to talk to him.

They moved the table back into the precise spot from which it had been pushed. They straightened the cut glass and porcelain and Majolica ware that had been displaced from the shelves in the corner of the room. She dusted everything carefully, wiping away all trace of the intruders and the fingerprint powder together.

At last, she nodded to him. "You sit down for a while. You look tired. I'll get us some coffee, and then I want to talk to you. I'm worried about something silly, and you can tell me I'm not as well as I pretend to be, and maybe I'll stop worrying. Then again, maybe I'll just keep right on but hold it in."

This was the time. He had learned to take advantage of every opportunity she gave him to help her with her long struggle. He sat in the stuffed plush armchair that still held the print of his grandfather's ample bottom; he slipped down into the depression, as always, feeling himself ridiculously slight and frail, compared with the burly Scotsman who had put together the heritage of the Frosts.

When Lily returned with the lacquered tray and two Haviland cups and saucers, the rose-sprigged pot, and the Irish linen napkins, he felt tears come to his eyes. That was the signal his mother had used, when she had something important to talk over with his father. They had known as children to go about their own affairs, leaving the adults to solve whatever strange problems haunted their distant world.

When the cups were filled, the steam rising from the flared shapes, the napkins properly placed on their laps, Lily took a sip, as if for courage. Then she set her saucer carefully on the big table and leaned forward, setting her elbows on her knees in the old tomboyish way her mother had disliked so much.

"Stony, I had a dream."

"I suspect we both had bad dreams, Lily. I tossed and turned, when I wasn't having nightmares." He knew this wasn't enough, and he waited again.

"It wasn't that sort of dream. I've had them before—dreamed things that really happened, later. But sometimes, if I realized what it was, what might happen, I have done things differently, and it has meant things turned out in a different way. I don't know—am I making it clear?"

"You mean that you dreamed, changed what you were going to do because of the dream, and nothing bad came afterward," he said. He didn't mention it, but he had done something of the sort himself.

"Yes. I dreamed that Martin killed me, the night before he killed that boy. So I went out early to the grocery store. When I came back, he was already after Sammy, and he killed him while I watched. The neighbors came before he could get me, too." She looked rather defiant, as if she expected him to laugh at the notion.

"So what was it you dreamed that frightened you?" he asked in his gentlest tone.

"I dreamed that either Martin or that man who looked

like him—killed you. And I had the strongest feeling that if we don't understand that can happen...we may regret it terribly.

"I want you to take this seriously, Stony. I want you to carry a weapon all the time. What have you got that you can carry without it seeming to be a weapon? It seems as if Grandfather had something sneaky, but I can't quite remember what it was."

Livingston felt a strange sensation go through him, half recognition, half comfort. She cared about him and worried about him. He'd wondered, as she worked through her long time of trauma, if she had time even to think of him at all. Now he knew.

"The rifle cane," he said, in a rather pedantic voice. "Grandfather bought it in 1910 from a bankrupt estate over in Louisiana. Single shot, rim fire, .32 caliber, grip shaped like the head of a dog. It looks like a walking stick, but it contains one round that can come as a very nasty surprise to anyone expecting to find a...helpless cripple who can't defend himself."

"Yes!" she said, leaning even farther in her chair. "I remember now; Gramma found me playing with it in their closet once, and took me out right then, loaded it, and made me fire it at the ash barrel. I'll never forget the cloud of ashes that flew in all directions when the slug hit it. Then she hid it away, and I barely remembered enough about it to bring it to mind. That's what you need, Stony. It wasn't displayed in the house—I'd remember if it had been."

"It's in my closet. For some reason, I always liked the thing—it reminded me of Grandfather. It's behind my garment bag, on the left side, if you want to go up and get it. We'll load it right now, if that will make you happier." He found himself strangely excited at the thought of carrying the cane, which would never be recognized for what it was except by another expert in antique firearms.

She was gone at once, and he heard her impatient steps crossing the landing, going up the second flight of steps, pattering down the worn carpet of the second-floor hall-way. He leaned back in the worn chair and looked at the ceiling, where two linked rings of discoloration, formed when the roof had leaked once when he was a child, still reminded him of the youngster he used to be.

The old house was sound. He had taken care of that, but he hadn't redone anything. He didn't care much for modern things, and Lily seemed not to mind. But perhaps he should have the roof checked again, before another rain. It seemed that the circles had a damp spot in the center of each.

The steps came tripping down the stairs again; Lily entered the parlor, holding the rifle cane carefully in both hands. The gutta percha that formed it was a bit dusty, and she wiped it with her dust cloth before handing it to him.

Livingston twisted the dog's-head grip, unlocking the mechanism from the cane's barrel. He pressed the latch, letting the spring zip forward. He blew the dust out and squeezed the grip, pulling the spring back into place, where he locked it with the latch again.

The barrel was also dusty. He sent Lily for his gun-cleaning kit and pulled the swab through by the tough string. When he looked through, the inside was shiny again.

The mechanism was so simple that there was nothing else to do except to load the thing. There were cartridges of all calibers in the breakfront, along with his loading equipment. Once the .32 cartridge was in place, the stock relocked onto the barrel, the cane became, once again, a respectable gentleman's support, never betraying its deadly contents. The weight was just right—not too much for a cane that could be carried comfortably. He rose, using it as a support, and moved around the room.

"I don't know why I haven't used this more," he said,

tapping briskly around the big table. "It's just the right length, and I could use it for a sort of trademark. It's old enough not to come under the Firearms Act, too, so I shouldn't be in too much trouble if I got caught with it."

"Wash wouldn't care," Lily said. She looked more relaxed, now.

"I travel a lot. But when I travel, I'm not likely to meet either Martin or his look-alike. So if I use it here at home, taking it with me for display, then I suspect it will work out rather well." He smiled at her, feeling an unaccustomed warmth.

They had lived together without quarreling but without overt affection for so long that it took him a while to realize what he felt as a remnant of that old childhood love they had shared.

"We're both crippled, you know?" he mused aloud. His own voice startled him, and he glanced up at Lily, afraid that he might have wounded her.

But she was nodding. "You're right. I have been crippled in my mind, you in your body, and we've been trying so hard not to show it that we haven't had the time to take care of each other properly. But I think that has changed, Stony.

"Maybe those nasty men did us a favor. We needed a shock, something harsh and painful, to wake us up. And now that we're awake, let's not go black to sleep. I want to keep alert, because that big man reminded me too much of Martin.

"Martin would come back and kill me, if he discovered he hadn't done the job completely the first time. You didn't know him, but I knew him entirely too well. I want to sleep with one eye open for a while."

Livingston had been trying to ignore his own intuition. He, too, had a feeling that the problem was far from over. "Why don't I call Shipp and see what they've discovered?" he asked, pulling himself up and balancing on the cane.

When Lucy Fowler answered, he was assaulted with questions. "Yes, we're both all right. No problem. I just wanted to find out if Shipp knows anything yet. They did find those fingerprints, and there should have been time to get word about the FBI files on them."

Lucy, of course, knew anything that the sheriff did. "The word came in about a half hour ago. Shipp was going to come out and talk with you, but he was called away to an accident. I can get it—yes, here it is, on the computer.

"The prints are those of Donald Crowley, white male, twenty-seven years of age, convicted in St. Tammany Parish five years ago of armed robbery, rape, and homicide in connection with the holdup of a convenience store and the capture of a hostage. One nasty customer, Stony."

"How in hell did he get out of prison so soon?" Livingston felt a helpless rage building in his chest. "With all those convictions, he should have been put away for good."

She sighed audibly. "You know how it goes. They appealed, and the appellate court found a tiny technical flaw in the first trial. A misplaced comma or something just as ridiculous. So they turned him loose, and now he's at it again. His twin, David, is just as bad a piece of work, but he has never been convicted, yet."

"Is there any information that might lead to the others? That big man that looked like Martin Fewell, for instance." He heard keys tapping. Then, "In prison, Crowley was boon companions with a fellow called Myron Duson. His people came from Louisiana, but he has kin all over southern Texas as well. He was in for extortion with the threat of violence. The picture they faxed to us looks quite a lot like Martin Fewell.

"They know, Shipp said, that he's been into a lot of things, from dope to prostitution to grand larceny, but he's been too slick to get sent up for more than a couple of years. And he got out early for good behavior."

She paused and cleared her throat. When she spoke, it was carefully, as if she didn't want to alarm him. "His M.O. is very simple, actually. He never leaves a witness alive."

"Damn!" Livingston found that he was gripping the phone with a hand suddenly damp with sweat. "I had the feeling—Lucy, I think Lily is in a lot of danger. What should we do?"

"I'm not the lawman around here, Stony. I just don't know. But when Wash gets back, I'll have him call or come out and talk to you both. We can't have you and your sister living in fear. If you need to leave the house for a while, do you have someplace to go?"

Livingston thought for a long moment. The only possibility was not one he fancied. "Well, yes, Lucy. But I'd like to put that off as long as possible. And I would like for it to be kept secret, even from you and the deputies, if you don't mind, so I won't mention where it is. You tell Wash to call. And thanks."

He turned from the phone, leaning against the breakfront. He felt suddenly dizzy, and Lily came to his side, concern on her face.

"You okay?" she asked, helping him sit again in the over-sized chair.

He managed a grin. "Of course. Just too much excitement, I think. Shipp will be out, probably late. We'll talk over what we need to do when he gets here, all right? I'm just not up to it right now."

To his relief, she nodded and went back to her polishing. There was no need to worry her more than she was already.

But that left Stony to worry alone.

THE GUNS OF LIVINGSTON FROST

CHAPTER SEVEN

WASHINGTON SHIPP

Wash got to his office early, after getting the input on the descriptions of the men who robbed the Frost home. He hadn't slept well, couldn't stop thinking about the attack on Lily Frost and the theft of her brother's guns. Both thoughts filled him with gloom.

He was glad he hadn't thrown that earlier interstate report away—he dug it out of the desk drawer where he had put it and read it over again. This almost had to be the same bunch mentioned there, the Duson bunch, and he hated to think of their being in his territory. The fact that Duson never left a witness alive was particularly troubling. He'd had only one conviction, because of his careful methods. Given that, there was a good possibility that he, at least, might come back to silence Lily.

Poor Lily. Life had dealt her a pretty bad hand, beginning with Martin Fewell. The Fewells had lived on a hardscrabble farm down near the Nichayac, back when Wash used to visit his grandparents on their farm deep in the river bottom country. His Aunt Libby knew Mrs. Fewell, as they were both devoted gardeners, but she carefully avoided knowing the old man.

"They's religious folks and they's mean folks, but

when you get both kinds together in one skin, you've got a really nasty kind of person," she had told his mother once when he was small.

Wash, quiet as usual, and listening with both ears, had found himself wondering how religious people could be mean, but he knew better than to open his mouth. When he was lucky, grown folks tended to forget he was there at all.

"Mister Fewell sure is religious, and that seems to make him particularly mean," his mother had said. "I was down that way and met Miz Fewell walkin' along the road. She had bruises down her arms and her face was a sight to see. Said she'd fell down the porch steps, but I know the shape of a fist-bruise. That old man'd been beatin' on her again."

Aunt Libby nodded solemnly. "The children say he knocks his young'uns round all the time. The girls are afeared to talk about it, but young Marty, he talks too much. They say he cusses his old man so as to make a sailor blush."

Unseen, Wash had nodded agreement. He had heard that himself. He knew he ought to feel sorry for a boy whose Pap beat him, but somehow he couldn't. Martin seemed to be as mean as his daddy, and tough as a bois d'arc root. He hit any child he could reach and lied with a straight face if the kid complained to his parents.

Wash had avoided the fellow all his life, and even now, as a lawman, he found himself frowning, just with thinking about him.

But the attacker hadn't been Martin Fewell! Just looked like him. With the descriptions and the fingerprint, surely he could get an I.D. on that one. Even as he thought that, Amy brought in a printout.

"Fingerprint identification," she said. "Con named Crowley, known associate of Myron Duson, the one they mentioned in those dispatches you had yesterday. What you want to bet they figured out a partnership while they were in stir?"

"It's a good guess, but at this point it's just that. We'll wait to find out more before we wind up our springs and go off into orbit." He placed the printout in a file along with the report and turned to the rest of the accumulation on his desk.

Every day was a long day for the Sheriff of Nichayac County.

THE GUNS OF LIVINGSTON FROST

CHAPTER EIGHT

MARTIN FEWELL

In twenty years, Martin Fewell had grown old. Not in years—he was only forty-nine—but physically and mentally. His craggy face was runneled with wrinkles that seemed to be caked with the dust of centuries, and his hair was a nondescript brown-gray. His husky frame, which had been misused so often in mistreating Lily and others, had shrunk on its bones, leaving his back humped and his skin hanging loosely at neck and belly.

He felt as old as God, he often thought, as he made his erratic way from town to town in the ten-year-old Chevy pickup that seemed to intend to last forever. Keeping it running and finding a way to feed himself kept him strapped for cash and working at penny-ante jobs to survive.

No longer did sheriffs and police chiefs automatically give him his walking papers when he came through town to post bills advertising the circus that was his present employer. He didn't even look threatening any more. Just dingy and down-at-heel. He often studied his image in the mirror and felt an emptiness where his old macho aggressiveness had been.

He often wondered what had become of Lily. When he

was sober and in a good mood, he had always known that she was the best thing he ever had going for him. Her gentleness, her attempts to keep him well fed and clothed, and her need for something stable in their lives had annoyed him often. Now he knew that he would give anything to undo the terrible series of actions that had turned her against him at last. He sighed as he stepped down from the pickup and took out the posters he must put up that day.

Being the advance man for a circus should have been interesting, but it was only more dog-work. And now, as he held a poster against a tree and readied the staple gun, there came a curious policeman, gesturing for him to stop.

"Something wrong, officer?" he asked. "The permits should have been arranged a week ago. Carroll Brothers Circus and Carnival."

"We'll check," the man said, taking him by the elbow and waltzing him toward the storefront housing the city hall. "You just come with me."

Damn! He thought. You watch—those bastards probably forgot the permits, and now I'll have to pay a fine and this will be another job gone into la-la-land.

He sat in an uncomfortable chair shaped like a wash tub, while the policeman went into the back room. There were few others there, and he could hear a radio droning the news in the adjoining city police office.

A name of a town caught his attention. "...men apprehended at five o'clock A.M. are suspected to be those wanted in a burglary and assault last evening near Templeton, Texas. Two others escaped into the darkness and their trail has not yet been found. It is thought that a stolen car, found abandoned later beside Highway 171, may have been used in avoiding arrest.

"The collection of Livingston Frost, noted dealer in antique firearms, was taken in the robbery, and his sister was injured. There is an all-points bulletin out in eastern Texas and western Louisiana for those suspects not yet apprehended.

"One suspect is tentatively identified as Myron Duson, present address unknown. His companion is still unknown, though he is described as being tall, heavy-set, and wearing a hat with a wide brim, which hides his face.

"Another robbery has been reported in Many, Louisiana, this one involving two teen-agers armed with switch-blades...."

Martin switched off his ears. Livingston Frost—his sister had to be the girl he knew. And her brother had been a wimpy little cripple.

Could he be a gun dealer? Antique guns? Probably. It was the sort of easy business a man like that might get into, though the subject of her brother's business had never come up during the time with Lily.

As he sat thinking, the officer returned. "No permits have been obtained," he said, his tone brusque. "Sorry, Mr. Fewell, but you'll have to leave your posters unposted. There's no fine, as you hadn't put one up, but I'd suggest you move on. Granger isn't a good town for itinerants."

Martin nodded and went back out to his truck. He'd never seen a hick town that was a good one for itinerants. He could say that he was an expert on the insides of shabby jails and the wrong sides of red-neck police and deputies who were long on muscle and short on brains.

The cop had followed him onto the street, and he turned suddenly and said, "Could you tell me how far it is to Templeton, Texas?"

The man looked puzzled for a moment. Then his face brightened. "Oh, yeah. Little town on the Nichayac River. I don't know in miles, but I figure about four and a half hours, driving the speed limit."

Martin tried to smile. "Thanks. Got folks over there, and I think I'll pay 'em a visit."

When he pulled away, the old truck rattling and groaning, the cop was still staring after him. Martin thanked his luck that it had been twelve years since his trial and the bad publicity when he'd been turned loose. Those country cops could figure out ways to hold you that would boggle the mind.

He turned west on Interstate 10. Lily didn't want to see him, he knew, but he had suddenly realized that he needed to see her. To say something to her.

Maybe just to tell her he was sorry. Not only for what he had done to her, but for what others like him had done as well.

THE GUNS OF LIVINGSTON FROST

CHAPTER NINE

ALISON FROST VERNIER

Allison Frost Vernier was ninety-one years old and still going strong. She had married late in life, and after taking that drastic step, she had been so absorbed in getting her house (and her somewhat bewildered husband) into order that she lost touch with her kinfolk in Templeton.

Their father had been her nephew, which made them somewhat distant both in age and consanguinity, and that made it easy for them to slip out of her immediate ken. When the phone rang, early on a rainy morning in late March, she expected it to be one of her many acquaintances who shared her passion for breeding registered English Setters.

But it was her great-nephew, Livingston. His voice was one she recognized only after some thought, for she missed his first words, her hearing not being as accurate as she pretended.

"Who?" She shook the receiver, as if that might clear up the tinny stream of words.

Again he spoke. "Aunt Allie, it's Livingston. Stony. You remember me—my grandfather was your brother. Lily and I haven't seen you in years, but surely you remember us!"

She detected in his voice something too much like desperation to be comfortable. "Of course I remember. I am not senile, Livingston, whatever anyone might say. And what might I do for you?" She was hoping devoutly that this was an idle chat, for she drove herself and everyone on her large farm with an intensity that brooked no interruptions.

She was always frantically busy and had little time for socializing, kin or no kin.

"We need...we need a place to hide, Aunt Allie."

She shook the phone again. Surely he'd said he needed a place to hide, and that simply could not be correct. "Repeat that. I thought I heard you say...."

"That I need to hide. Yes. Or rather, Lily needs to. We were robbed, and the ringleader of the criminals never leaves a witness alive. Lily saw him. Aunt Allie, we've got to find someplace where he can't find us. Just for a while. Will Uncle Louis mind?"

Had it been that long? She sighed. "Louis died two years ago, Livingston. And if you need a refuge, of course you can stay with me. I hope you don't mind working in the kennels a bit—we are short-handed, right now, and extra help would be a godsend.

"Is Lily...?"—she paused, trying to think of a tactful way to ask the question—"...is Lily feeling up to helping out, too?"

His voice reassured her. "Lily has pulled out of her problem, almost all the way. That's why I want to get her completely away, so none of this new mess can send her into a tailspin.

"She works like a Trojan. Keeps house and cooks for me, works in the garden. She can help too, Aunt Allie. I'm the one who has a bit of trouble getting around."

"Oh, yes. The polio. I keep forgetting. Nevertheless, you must both come to me at once. If someone is threatening to kill my niece, we must hide her well and protect her intelligently. I will not brook anyone threatening my family, no matter what.

"Bring some of your guns, Stony. All I have is a twenty-gauge shotgun loaded with birdshot and a .38 pistol." Already her busy mind was arranging rooms, laying out plans to keep both of her kinspeople occupied enough to avoid thinking about their situation. The dogs were important to her, but she had never become so attached to them that she valued them above people.

"We can come tomorrow, if that's all right?" Stony sounded relieved.

"Come at once, if you want. Can't have my niece murdered by a burglar, now can we?" She stretched her arthritic knee and set about flexing it, ignoring the pain as she kept it mobile. "You come right on, and I will have things ready when you arrive."

"Thanks, Auntie. And I'm sorry about Uncle Louis. I didn't know." He sounded genuinely regretful.

"My own fault, boy. I should have written you, but somehow, what with the estate and the dogs and everything, I never even wrote his own sister, down in Lafayette. I'll do that right now, before I forget again."

She wrote the note before rising from the telephone table, scribbling an abrupt and yet heartfelt message inside a note-card and stamping it for mailing. But her mind was not entirely on her task. She was thinking of Lily, who had been a drug addict and a runaway.

The child had been dreamy and hard to handle, it was true. But Allison felt rather certain that her great-niece's adventure in her youth had been caused by the sort of romantic nature she recognized in herself.

Her own marriage had been as unexpected and intense, as shocking to those who knew her as a reclusive and intellectual thirty-year-old, as Lily's abrupt departure had been to her own family. Only a matter of generations had made a difference in the way that trait had cropped out.

She rose, forcing her back straight, and made her recalcitrant knees march toward the kitchen, where her friend and long-time employee now reigned. "Maggie!" she called, as she stumped into the room, "We're going to have company. My brother's grandchildren are coming for a visit."

Not for a moment did she consider letting Maggie know the reason for that visit. The girl had, at seventy-two, settled down a bit, but she still was prone to excited ditherings over what had to be taken as the normal dangers and dilemmas of life.

"The little boy and girl? Miss Allie! What a treat! They must be grown by now." Maggie's coffee-colored cheeks stretched into a grin.

"And then some," Allison said, her tone gruff. "Tell Sissy to make up the two front rooms over the south porch. Livingston is lame—you remember he had polio, back when he was a child? So see that the little stair-rail lift is working, to take him up the stairs."

Maggie looked smug. "Been wanting to fix it up so's you can use it your own self," she mumbled toward the piecrust she was rolling paper-thin on the marble slab topping the work table.

Allison was not that deaf. "I heard that! The day I am too lame to climb my own stairs, I shall move my bedroom down into the sun parlor and forget the house has those upstairs rooms. Until then, you just do as I ask and don't try to make me feel old!"

* * * * * * *

The day whisked past, and by the time the Toyota pulled to a stop in the drive, everything had been done to her specifications, although she had spent most of that period exercising the dogs. Her staff, rare in these modern times, was middle-aged to elderly, determined to last at least as long as she did, and devoted to their crotchety employer. Things got done at Allison Vernier's breeding farm, and others in the business could only envy her.

She showered and changed. When the newcomers stepped out of the little car, she went slowly down the steps to meet them, her gait nicely suited to the condition of her knees. "Stony! Lily!" She stretched out her hands to them, noting with unexpected pain that both now showed their age, and detecting the effort with which her great-nephew forced his thin limbs to move as he came to meet her.

"Aunt Allie." He took her hand lightly into his, and she realized that he, too, knew the agony of a tight hand-clasp on meeting a stranger unfamiliar with arthritic joints.

Lily stood there, tall and somewhat awkward, her expression uncertain. Though she was every day of thirty-nine, she still had the look of an awkward teenager. Allison put an arm about her waist (being too short to reach any higher) and gave her a little hug.

"Welcome, children. It has been too long—and we are the last of the Frosts. We must do this more often and with happier reasons." She reached to take her cane from the spot where she had leaned it against the porch railing, and they moved together back into the house.

It was strange, she thought, as she ushered them into the sitting room and placed them on either side of her deep chair. She had all but forgotten these two in her busy round of tasks.

Yet now that she saw them, she felt a surge of protective possessiveness go through her. They were her own flesh and blood, her brother's descendants. Anyone threatening them would have Allison Frost Vernier to contend with!

But she made herself relax, smiling and chatting and helping her guests to lose a bit of the tension that was so evident in their bodies and faces. By the time Maggie came with coffee in the best china cups and plates of thin tea-cakes, they had all begun to talk easily together in the faded splendor of the sitting room, with the last of the sunset dyeing the sky scarlet beyond the French windows. While Livingston described the burglary, she watched Lily. According to her infrequent communications with Livingston, the girl had been extremely frightened and terribly passive after her return home. Allison felt certain she had been desperately mistreated by the man with whom she eloped.

That had, to an extent, disgusted her, for she felt that any Frost worth her salt would have left the son-of-a-bitch, or killed him, or both.

But now Lily seemed reasonably relaxed. She even described the men who broke into the house, though in years past she would have left all the talking to her brother. Her eyes had lost the look of terror that lived there for so long, though by rights this new danger should have left her terrified.

Allison found herself growing angry. What right had a bunch of toughs to come pushing in and upset the recovery of this niece of hers, who had lived through so much pain and fear?

"Did you bring some guns?" she asked Stony, when Lily was done. "I called the sheriff after we talked, and he said he'd do what he could, but this is a poor county, and he hasn't enough deputies to set a guard or anything like that."

"I shipped them UPS," her nephew said. "A Toyota isn't built for carrying long guns. But I brought this one with me—it isn't good for a fire-fight, but it can surprise the heck out of one person, one time."

He offered her his cane, and she chuckled as she recognized her brother's rifle cane. "Good thinking. I wish I had one myself. You just use that cane as if it were nothing but a walking stick, and I'll load my .38—you remember it, Stony?—and keep it in my pocket. We'll surprise the hell out of anybody who thinks he's going to run over us!"

Somewhat to her surprise, Alison felt a surge of excitement. It had been too long since she had been faced with danger, and she felt her blood warming, her heartbeat picking up its pace. Not since that long-ago feud with the crooks running her parish had she needed to prepare for war, and it amused her to find that she was no more civilized now than she had been forty years ago.

THE GUNS OF LIVINGSTON FROST

CHAPTER TEN

SEPTIEN CARREFOURS

Septien Carrefours was not a wicked man. He had always assured himself that he was a thief—the best in the business—but not someone that the old grandmères would use to frighten children. Now he was growing uncomfortable.

Myron Duson was a violent man; there was no getting around that fact. He had the reputation for being one who left no living witnesses, though Septien had discounted that when he was told about it. Surely nobody would be so foolish as to kill without a driving need. But this first job with Duson had shaken that assurance.

The man had a flair—that was undeniable. Yet this particular job had gone sour from the moment they walked into that old house and found the skinny woman making bread in the kitchen.

Septien had a weakness for tall, slender women, and he particularly liked domestic ones. He had been secretly relieved when it turned out that David Crowley hadn't bashed in her skull after all.

When he discovered that the guns were almost worthless, it had filled him with a sort of wicked amusement. Duson was so cock-sure, so domineering, and so harsh that this proof of his fallibility was something Septien savored. Nobody was as good as Myron thought he was.

At that moment, Septien had been ready to bail out of the deal and go his own way. A thief with his expertise was always in demand, and he didn't have to stand hitched with this man who seemed, more and more, to be crazy.

This was a proof of that. After getting away clean from that disaster behind them, was he sane enough to head for the tall timber? Anyone with sense would have done that.

But no! He was going back to Texas to try to kill that woman again. It made no sense to Septien; he wanted badly to stop the car, get out, and walk away across the flat fields alongside Interstate 10.

He had, however, a nasty feeling that Duson would shoot him in the back if he did. Whatever his scruples, Septien had no desire to die. Life was good, and his Emilie waited patiently for him to come back still again to Grosse Tête, down in the swamp country.

She was, he realized, much like that woman Duson wanted to kill. Perhaps that was why he objected so strenuously to the present job in hand.

That made another good reason to want to slip away from this madman and make a trail for Cajun country. But he drove and drove, with Duson sitting, sleepless and wordless, beside him, making the incredible return from Alexandria, where they had retrieved money from a secret stash Duson had left there. Duson was planning what? Septien would have given a lot to know just what was going on behind those flat, cold eyes. Still, he knew he was going to have to step carefully, if he was going to get away from this with a whole skin. The first step was to disable the car.

They stopped, of course, for gas and food and restrooms, from time to time. Septien had always been meticulous about checking the oil in any car he drove, owned or stolen, for he had seen too many careful planners brought down by a lack of attention to such details.

This was the fourth stolen car since that first one in which they had escaped the capture of the van. It was an unobtrusive gray Olds—an eighty-nine model, old enough not to arouse attention, and yet still powerful and dependable. He hoped its former driver had survived the crack on the head Duson had delivered when they liberated the car in Alexandria.

He had developed his usual affection for the vehicle, as it purred along the Interstate to Lake Charles, turned north toward DeRidder on Highway 171, and sped northward. When they were far from any convenient source of stolen cars, his planning began to go into effect. The gas was low, as he had intended.

"We mus' stop at the nex' Mom and Pop station. We need gas, and I got to stretch or I be going to get too stiff for anything," he said, his tone casual.

Duson grunted. He had been dozing for the past half-hour. He had, Septien hoped, no suspicion that his henchman was getting restless.

"I stop at Ragley. Little place ahead. Get plenty travelers through, so they won' notice us, I think. You stay in de car, jus' in case.

"Right there, you know, there be a state road, turn off toward the wes'—save us gas and there ought to be no patrolmen there at all. Nothin' out there but pine tree for miles." He glanced aside at Duson.

"Sounds good. Just do it and get on with it," Duson growled. "The sooner we get that bitch quieted down for good, the sooner we can go about our business. Just let me sleep!" He hitched himself around, put his hat over his face, and went silent.

Just right. If the car happened to go dead somewhere between Ragley and Merryville, there'd be nothing to steal for miles. Duson might get rattled enough to give him a chance to slip away into the woods, and once among the pines, Septien Carrefours could not be caught by any man, unless he wanted to be.

* * * * * * *

Ragley consisted of one store and a sign pointing toward the state road to Merryville. Septien pulled to a stop beside the pumps and got out to stretch. Duson didn't move, and a muffled snort told him that the madman was sleeping.

A cheerful-looking old fellow came out of the store, accompanied by the tinkle of an old fashioned bell over the door, and asked, "What kin I do for you?"

"Fill up de gas, will you, while I check de oil?" Septien pulled the hood latch and went around to open the hood. While there, he quietly punctured the oil line, punching a carefully gauged hole that would let the oil escape slowly enough to allow them to travel a certain distance.

When the tank was filled, the hood went down softly, so as not to wake his passenger, and Septien doled out bills into the old man's hand. The fellow didn't seem a bit curious.

With a nod, he got back into the car and cranked it carefully—Duson would not hesitate to confiscate the ancient pickup truck parked at the side of the store building if the car showed early signs of demise. The man had never learned anything about cars, and that was an ignorance that was about to cost him dearly.

Septien turned onto the road. To his surprise, it had been black-topped since he last detoured in that direction. That might mean a bit more traffic than the road used to carry, but he intended to leave this vehicle before they hit Merryville, that was for sure and certain.

* * * * * * *

It didn't take long to pass all the houses that were strung loosely along the road near the hamlet. Then they were in pine timber country. Cut over time after time, the young trees were coming back strongly, and he smelled the pine straw scent with pleasure.

It was spring! The woods were beginning to leaf out, the stands of hardwoods showing a mist of green and the dogwoods beginning to gleam with white among the dark tree trunks. It would be no problem to make his way to a suitable highway, going as straight through the woods as any arrow, guided by his sure instinct for direction.

The miles passed, and he almost dozed himself, for the road was contained between walls of trees, without any break to make for interest. And then a deer darted from the hedgerow on the right, directly in front of the car.

Septien jammed on his brakes, sending Duson flopping onto the dash, his head thumping on the windshield.

"You damn fool! You trying to kill me?" Duson was rubbing his head, looking about with the dazed expression a sudden awakening brings to a sleeper.

"Better bump your head than bash our radiator on a deer!" Septien pointed off to the left, where a blur of brown and a pale scut were disappearing into the trees.

"Well, start the goddam car and get us out of here!" Naturally, the engine had died, much to Septien's satisfaction. The oil gauge, which had been indicating trouble for miles now, died with the engine. When he tried the ignition, nothing happened—the thing was probably frozen up tight.

"What's the problem?" Duson opened his door and went around to the hood.

Septien smiled as he pulled the latch. Duson wouldn't notice anything less than an engine that was entirely missing. "We see," he said.

Standing beside his partner in crime, Septien bent over

to peer into the workings of the motor. Oil was spattered all over everything, stinking to high heaven, but of course Duson didn't know that such a condition wasn't normal.

"I can't tell you. I see nothin' wrong, but this, it is a car I don' know. Maybe there was something wrong when we take her, eh? It finally come apart, and leave us stranded here. Miles from anyplace!" He managed to make his voice sound despairing.

"Where's the nearest town?" Duson sounded ready to kill, and Septien stepped back.

"Maybe five—six miles. Not too far to walk. I do it many time back home."

He knew with wicked amusement that Duson thought feet were made for the purpose of displaying expensive shoes. The idea of walking more than a couple of blocks on them would turn him pale. And it did.

"Six miles?" The man's tone was furious. "Septien, when I told you to steal a car that wouldn't be noticeable, I thought you knew enough not to lift a junker. Six miles!"

He turned back the way they had come. "How far back to Ragley?"

"Ten mile, maybe."

"Did we pass any farms along the way?"

"Nothin' but the pine tree for a long time now."

"Shit!"

It was all the Cajun could do to keep from grinning openly. But he said, "Maybe there be a house up ahead. We gettin' closer to de nex' town than you think. You want to go see while I check out dis car? Maybe I can fin' what is wrong, while you go."

Muttering something obscene, Duson trudged away without answering. If there were a house up ahead, Septien pitied anyone living there. The mood Duson was in, he would have pitied a bear or a panther that met him on the road.

But that was not his concern. He would have time to

get well into the woods before the madman returned, and Duson in the woods would be even more inept than he was under the hood of a car. The Cajun waited until a long curve up ahead took the departing shape out of sight.

Then Septien reached into the car for the bag of candy bars he always carried when he traveled. This was wet country, and he'd find water, he knew, though he also knew that it wouldn't be that long before he emerged onto some road that would supply a ride or a vulnerable car to take him back toward Grosse Tête and his waiting Emilie.

Before Duson had gone a mile, the Cajun was strolling through the stand of young pine on the south side of the road. In another twenty minutes, he risked a snatch of song. He was free of Duson at last!

His feet covered miles of pine plantings, as he thought with wicked glee about Duson's future. Serve him right, he thought, if that lady there in Templeton kill him dead!

But that was no longer any of his concern.

THE GUNS OF LIVINGSTON FROST

CHAPTER ELEVEN

MYRON DUSON

The asphalt road was already sticky in the March sunlight, and the damp left from the rain the night before filled the air with a steamy heat. Duson was not in a good mood.

The catnaps he had taken while riding had not rested him, and the demise of the Olds infuriated him. Carrefours was a fool! He had no confidence that the mechanic could fix whatever ailed the car, no matter how long he tinkered with it.

Duson had no intention of wasting another thought on the idiot. Let him stay there in the heat, under the hood of the vehicle. Let him be caught and be damned to him! He knew nothing about Duson, for Myron had taken care not to inform any of his henchmen about anything important in his life. Myron Duson intended to go on alone. He had no need of others to help him finish the job he had begun. If only he could locate a farm, someplace along this god-forsaken road, he would find transportation, and that was the only thing he needed at the moment.

The pines on either hand seemed to hold in the heat, and he took off his jacket and folded it neatly over his arm. His hat was not wide-brimmed enough to keep the sun off his neck, but it helped a bit as he trudged onward, scanning the roadsides ahead for any hint of a driveway.

Forty-five minutes later, he saw a break in the bushes along the fence line, with a muddy drive leading away from the asphalt. Rounding a curve, he could see big trees growing some distance from the road, and beneath their shade huddled a tin-roofed frame house.

He almost grinned, but he saved the energy for later. That would be the break he needed, and he must make it work for him. Nobody must know that he was coming until he sized up the situation.

He turned aside and climbed through a tight, barbed wire fence, catching himself painfully several times on its barbs before he made it all the way through and emerged on the other side. A field of brush and weeds lay between him and the house now, screening his approach, if he stooped and took reasonable care.

He was no woodsman, but he had learned by necessity to move across country. In time, he found himself at the back of a neat yard, where stalks of spring jonquils still stood stiffly under japonica bushes. There was no sign of anyone about, though a rusty pickup sat in a shed, which was a tin roof held up by four untrimmed posts, weathered to a satiny gray.

He ducked under a low sycamore limb and moved across a flowerbed toward the kitchen door, which was screened by a big dogwood. As he came around the bush, an old woman popped through into the back yard, holding a pan of scraps and calling, "Here, kitty-kitty!" at the top of her voice.

She saw him before he could reach her side, and her mouth opened. He didn't wait to learn whether a greeting or a scream was about to come out of it.

He hit her expertly at the side of the neck. When she went down, legs jerking reflexively, he leaned over and methodically crushed her skull with one of the whitewashed rocks from the edge of the path.

A gruff roar interrupted him, and he straightened to meet the assault of a man who was charging him with a crutch held like a spear. The gray ruffle of hair stood straight up on the old man's head, and his eyes were wild with fury and grief.

It was no great trick to demolish this one as well. No witness had ever lived to testify against Myron Duson. No witness except a single skinny woman in Texas.

Once he was certain there was nobody else around the place, he went through the house, searching for money or weapons or anything else that might be useful. He found a hoard of dimes in a fruit jar—not worth taking, he decided. He located an ancient ten-gauge shotgun whose load had corroded in its chamber. Worse than no good.

He did find a copy of *Sports Afield* with a five-dollar bill marking a place in it. Turning through to see if more bills might be inside, he found a familiar name staring at him.

ALLISON FROST VERNIER, breeder extraordinary, was the caption beneath a photo of an elderly woman standing in a run among a half-dozen English setters. An accompanying article was evidently about her breeding kennels and the success of her setters in field trials.

That was the name of those people in Templeton. A coincidence, perhaps, but Duson had not become the feared name it was through ignoring hunches. He noted the location of that farm. Might be a handle on the gun dealer, he thought. You never knew.

When he was done and had finished off a superb custard pie and a quart of milk from the refrigerator, he went out and searched the man's body for the pickup keys. To his amazement, however, he found the keys in the ignition, the door unlocked, and the vehicle ready to roll. What sort of place was this, where people could leave things so unsecured? But he didn't worry about that.

Instead, he put the thing in gear and rolled away westward in a cloud of smelly blue smoke. Once he reached civilization, he knew he could find a decent car. This one would last, he hoped, as long as he needed it. If it didn't, there were always other cars to take and other owners to delete.

THE GUNS OF LIVINGSTON FROST

CHAPTER TWELVE

WASHINGTON SHIPP

Washington Shipp was not easy in his mind. The Frosts were well away, staying with a relative. Only he and Amy, the dispatcher, knew where they were, and that should have reassured him, but for some reason he kept thinking about the man who had looked so much like Martin Fewell.

He had a gut feeling he wasn't through with that gun-stealing bastard, no matter that he had been stopped and almost apprehended across the Louisiana line. Two of his henchmen were in custody, not talking as yet, but the time would come when they would, he felt certain.

For that reason, he asked Amy to keep a special file of any bulletins issued in Louisiana, particularly ones concerning stolen cars, assaults, or burglaries. He hadn't realized how much paperwork that would entail, but he doggedly plowed through the morning's stack, watching for anything that rang his internal alarm.

Beside him was a large map of the East Texas-Western Louisiana area, and he had circled the point at which the van and two of its riders had been caught. Now he was plotting the spots at which cars had been stolen, beginning with one that had disappeared only a couple of blocks from the place where Duson and his henchman had disappeared. It was amazing how many vehicles had been stolen in Louisiana in the past day and a half.

He worked for an hour, blessedly uninterrupted by any local catastrophe worse than a cow in Mrs. Blasingame's garden. When he was done, the map was fairly well dotted with marks, but he could see that three of them lay in a direct line south and east along Interstate 10.

That was a boggler, for the pair might be heading toward New Orleans, where they could disappear easily and permanently. Still, his instinct said otherwise. "They turned west again," he muttered, staring at the map. "I'd bet my life on it."

Amy interrupted him with another bulletin. This one had brought a flush of excitement to her round face.

"Here's one from right across the line. An old couple was found yesterday afternoon near Merriville, Louisiana, beaten to death. Their house was ransacked and their pickup was stolen. A red Chevy, 1973 model, rusty, dent in right front fender. The license number is probably no good, now, but here it is." She thrust the papers into his hands and watched his face as he read.

Shipp felt a chill go down his spine. This was right. This was it. He had known the predator was coming back to make sure of his kill, and here was the trace he had been waiting for. The brutality of the crime convinced him that it must be Duson's work.

"Here's something else," said Amy, handing him another bulletin. "They found one of the stolen cars a couple of miles east of the murder site. The engine was frozen up, and the oil line had been perforated. "The local sheriff thinks that only one man committed the murders, for it had rained the night before and only a single set of tracks crossed the flowerbed at the back of the house. There wasn't a mark on the mud in the driveway except the tracks where the pickup went out."

He nodded. "That means the other one has left. He was an expert mechanic, from what I can gather, so if that oil line was holed, he did it on purpose. Now, where is he going? Not here, or he'd have come ahead with Duson. We may be able to scratch him off our list, but that doesn't do us any good. He wasn't the dangerous one."

"Here's the rest," she said.

He looked at the report she handed him. "Fingerprints found on the hood latch of the abandoned car matched those of Myron Duson, of Beaumont, Texas, convicted felon now wanted in Texas for robbery and assault, and Septien Carrefours, Grosse Tête, Louisiana, known car thief and associate of Maurice Boulangère, fence and dealer in stolen goods, New Orleans. Six arrests. No convictions."

He looked up at Amy. "Our boys," he said, his tone soft. "Headed this way, at least as far as Duson is concerned. We'd better stake out the Frost house. He'll go there for sure."

"Who can be spared?" she asked. "Lambert has been sick with the flu. Joseph went out to see about that cow in the garden, but when he gets back he's supposed to take night duty tonight. Both our late shift people are supposed to be in Austin tomorrow to testify in that DWI/vehicular homicide case."

"Damn!" Why was it that when you most needed manpower, everyone was out of pocket? Wash chewed at his thumbnail, thinking hard.

"Amy, could you stay here tonight and use the cot in the office, just in case anything comes in that needs handling? I could stake out the Frost house myself. That would leave Joseph free to patrol, and he could come if I needed him. Okay?"

She might groan a bit, but he knew she loved to fill in, when there was a need. She fancied herself a policewoman, he knew, when she could forget her age and her arthritic knees.

"He's on his way," he said, looking down at the map.
"From Merryville, he could have driven right here into the
county before dark last night and be hidden out already.
We'd better be on the watch for him. You call Joseph and
tell him the drill."

The day went slowly, after that, filled with paperwork.
From time to time, Wash looked up at the clock and wondered where Myron Duson was, what he was planning,
and how he would go about ambushing the bastard, if he
came to the Frost house that night. He didn't, of course,
know Duson. That meant he would have to be extremely
cautious.

But Washington Shipp knew to be cautious. If he got
himself into bad trouble, his wife Jewel would kill him for
sure.

THE GUNS OF LIVINGSTON FROST

CHAPTER THIRTEEN

MARTIN FEWELL

Martin had been driving for hours. His neck was stiff, and his back was cramped, and he needed to pee something awful. The hunch that was sending him westward, along the irregular jogs and windings of Highway 190, was still strong enough to keep him from stopping often, and he put such pauses off until he had to get gasoline.

Only when he had crossed the Texas line did he feel sufficiently at ease to pull over into a logging track beside the highway to relieve himself. To his disgust, there was a shabby pickup truck already pulled up, out of sight of the road behind him. Somebody hunting, he figured, though whatever it was, it was probably illegal in the spring.

He looked about, but nobody was in sight. Then he got out and stretched the cramps out of his joints. A short trip behind a clump of young pine trees got rid of another problem, and he went back to get into his pickup, which, while it was no Porsche, was still better than the wreck blocking the road.

Something made him stop. His old instincts, long dormant, suddenly waked, making him spin on his heel while ducking and letting his reflexes take over. His fist thudded into a hard belly while he still felt the breeze of the blow that had just missed his head. Then he was trying with desperate strength to hold down his assailant.

The man beneath him was as big as he was, harder and younger. Surely he was no match for the nasty tricks Martin had spent a lifetime in learning, in and out of prison.!

Yet he was. Martin fought him all the way, tripping him, eye-gouging, trying for a knee in the groin, but the fellow knew how to counter them all. This was an ex-con, without any doubt.

At last the attacker jerked free of him and hurled himself into the pickup, in which Fewell had left the keys. With a roar, the truck started, and before the older man could reach it, the driver slammed it into reverse and disappeared in a cloud of mud spatters.

Fewell stood in the quiet of the pine woods, his anger growing by the minute. That bastard hadn't given him a chance, just swung and hoped to kill. He'd met too many of the sort in his criminal career to mistake that. And now he was off in the only thing Fewell owned in all the world, outside of his few clothes, which were in his old suitcase in the camper.

The roar of the engine disappeared westward up 190. Well, by god, he wasn't one to stand around and let someone take off with his property.

He turned to the stranded truck and looked inside. Well-kept seats, but old. The body was rusty and dented. He opened the hood and peered into the engine. It smelled hot, but he didn't think it had seized up. Probably the thing was slow and rattly, and its driver had just decided to take the next thing that came along, when it got hot.

It was his own fault for turning off the highway. If he hadn't, that bastard would have snared somebody in a good car with some hard luck story out on the main road, and would be going west in style. Probably, if his methods held true, leaving the owner dead in a ditch.

He checked the gauges. There wasn't much gas left.

The oil pressure wavered around, once he got the engine started, but it settled down at last. It needed water, and he knew he'd better fill the radiator soon, but he thought he could nurse it along. There was a Mom and Pop grocery and station a few miles up the road, he remembered.

He intended to make it. That character might think he'd left Martin Fewell on foot, but he didn't know his man. He'd follow him across Texas, if he had to, just to get his own back. The little money in his pocket would buy gas and oil, and if he had to do without food for a while, he'd done that before.

He crept backward out of the logging track, looked both ways carefully, and backed onto the highway. Nobody was in sight. He pulled off in low, feeling out each gear as he shifted, making sure there was nothing badly wrong with the vehicle he now drove.

By the time he reached the store, the radiator was boiling again, but a fill of water and five dollars worth of gas seemed to settle the truck down pretty well. He got an extra can of oil, just in case the thing burned a lot. Then he set off in pursuit of the hijacker.

That sapsucker might think he was tough, but Martin Fewell had invented tough, and he intended to use every bit of it when he found the hijacker.

THE GUNS OF LIVINGSTON FROST

CHAPTER FOURTEEN

MYRON DUSON

He was losing his touch! Even as he pulled away from the scene of his latest disaster, Myron was fretting about that.

Out of his last four encounters, two of the victims had survived. That was a bad average—the sort that could get a man sent to Huntsville for that lethal injection they thought was so humane.

He had no intention of getting caught and even less of dying. But that old guy back there in the woods had been a tough son-of-a-bitch. Learned his stuff in a place with barred windows, he'd bet his life on that.

Just getting away from him uninjured had been a pretty hard thing to do. Killing him would have been something that Myron wasn't quite certain he could have accomplished. Not without more hassle than he was willing to risk.

The truck he drove was, however, many cuts above the clunker he had stolen after killing the old couple. It had been taken care of, that was clear. As he rattled along the newly widened highway toward Jasper, he watched the oil gauge. Septien had taught him that much at least. But it sat steady, and the gas gauge was what he found he must watch most closely. That truck guzzled gasoline as if it were free.

He hadn't all that much money with him. He'd depended on being paid for the Frost collection, when he delivered the guns, and his bit left with Linda in Alexandria hadn't been a lot. That damned Bollivar! But he shook away the thought. Done was done, and there was no point in worrying about it, for Bollivar was no threat to him.

No, the woman: she was the threat. And that man back there, who was still alive to yell assault and robbery when he made it to a town. He had never left so many loose ends before, and Myron was rattled at the thought that his magic touch was failing him.

He passed a highway patrol car, but the driver paid no heed to him. So. There hadn't been a complaint filed yet. Maybe he'd hurt that old buzzard enough so that he would lie there in the woods and die? That was wishful thinking. He knew the man had come nearer injuring him than the other way around. That sucker had taken his lumps in a prison yard, or Myron was no expert.

He pulled into Jasper and filled up at a big Exxon station on the corner where two main highways crossed. He watched his speed. He stopped at every sign and didn't slide through. He didn't want another hick town law to impede him in his business.

When he pulled out again, heading northwest to avoid Toledo Bend Lake, he was a model of propriety. But when he turned on State Highway 63, he sped up a bit. He wanted to get into Templeton just after dark.

He'd find a place to stay, keeping completely out of sight. When it was really late and the burg had rolled up its sidewalks, he would go out to that big old house and he'd finish the job Crowley had started.

He stopped at a café and ate before dark. He idled over coffee, watching traffic whiz past on the road, waiting until it was that lazy hour when everyone was at supper and the police'd had a long day but hadn't been relieved for the evening. When he was satisfied that everything was to his liking, he paid his tab and got back into the pickup.

Maybe it had been best to drive a working man's truck, looking sober and respectable. If he'd lifted a Lincoln, which he'd hoped to do, that would have been too flashy and noticeable. Regretfully, he decided that he would have to allow his efforts at a hitch-hiker's hard luck story to go to waste.

There was a flea-bag motel outside the Templeton city limits. He checked in, using the name he found on the registration in the pocket of the truck: Martin Fewell. Sounded solid and dull. Probably that tough back in the pine woods had stolen the truck himself, for he hadn't acted like a respectable citizen. They froze and let you slaughter them like sheep.

He was tired. He didn't like to drive, and he heartily cursed Carrefours for letting that comfortable Olds go sour on them. But he had chosen to come on without his driver, and he couldn't blame anyone but himself.

He lay on the chenille bedspread, still wearing his shoes, and turned on the TV. There was a news item about the murder in Louisiana, and to his horror he heard his name being mentioned. Fingerprints! He'd wiped everything, always. Compulsively!

They also mentioned Septien, but that was no comfort. Where had he left his prints? He had wiped the door handle, the dash, the seat cover, the outside of the doorframe. He always did that.

And then he thought of it. When he touched the hood. Someplace there, he had left a print he didn't realize was on it. A hidden place...the latch under the hood? That had to be it!

He was going soft. His skill was slipping, and his knack was dulling with age and over-use. He had to get back on track, or he would be a goner. He shut off the tube and turned on his side. He must sleep now. His interior timer would wake him when the night was at the correct point in its progress. He knew he could rely on that, if nothing else.

Tonight would see him back on track. Tonight would turn his career around, for good and all. With that thought, he dozed off, secure in his control of the future.

THE GUNS OF LIVINGSTON FROST

CHAPTER FIFTEEN

WASHINGTON SHIPP

Wash yawned, but he didn't move. His youth spent hunting in the river bottoms had trained him well for stalking men. The shelter of the Chinese holly was thick, the glossy leaves forming a prickly barrier between him and the light that Frost had left burning in the utility room off the back porch. He didn't want a rustle or a shiver of branches to betray his presence.

There had been no sign of anyone in the grounds, but that didn't mean Duson might not be within arm's reach of him. Wash had learned that in an even harsher school than prison. The forests along the Nichayac could be crawling with gators, moccasins, or cougars, and you never knew until it was too late. Worse than those were the illegal hunters, who would kill you without a thought or a backward glance.

He let out his breath silently and swiveled his eyes in their sockets, keeping a constant sweeping watch on the space around the back door of the Frost home. There was a feeling of tension in the air.

The mockingbird that had been going through his repertory in the tall sycamore beside the back porch was quiet now. Even the first timid peepers of spring had stilled their shrill voices, and there was only the sound of a light breeze whispering through the sharp-angled leaves of his sheltering holly.

Shipp had developed an instinct, back there in his youth, that had saved his life more than once. He knew, somehow and with some sense that wasn't physical, when a poisonous snake was sharing his hiding place. He'd felt impending dangers many times, even though no sound betrayed them and not even his elders were warned of their presence. Now he felt there was someone on the other side of the holly. Someone's ears strained at the night, trying to detect anything that didn't fit into the picture. Someone's breath was being controlled with great care, even as he was managing his own so as not to betray his presence.

He felt the tension in those other, invisible muscles. He understood on a primitive level the wariness and the caution of that other one, who even now thought he was stalking his prey.

Thinking of Lily Frost, of his own wife, safely at home with the boy, Wash eased his weight onto his left foot. The dried holly leaves, accumulating for years beneath the huge twists of branches, made no sound, for he brought the weight to bear slowly, steadily, and without the possibility of crunching. The branches swept softly past his shoulders, and there was no scrape of leaf against cloth.

As carefully as if he were about to face a cougar in the depths of the forest, he moved out of his nook and around the large bush. He expected at any moment to see the dark shape of his adversary.

There was a sudden blink of the dim light. A solid body had passed across its faint beam. Alarmed, he moved forward, his forty-five in hand, but the watcher was gone, vanished into the thick growth tangling the acreage around the house. Taking out his flash, the lawman examined the ground about the holly bush. There was a scuffed spot, as if big feet had rested in the same place for some time.

There was a skid mark, where the quarry had taken off like a scalded cat. He sank back on his heels and stared thoughtfully into the multiple shadows of the trees. This was a man with the instincts of a cat. He knew, just as Wash knew, when there was an enemy at hand.

They had waited, one on either side of the stickery complex of holly, trying to find what it was that had set off their inner warnings. Almost at the same moment, they had decided to move.

Shipp shivered. He didn't like feeling as if he were somehow akin to that dangerous creature shaped like a man. But he knew, deep inside, that he now understood Myron Duson far better than he had ever thought he might.

Sighing, he went to the back door and used the key Stony had left with him. He had to see if Duson had made it inside, though now he wondered if he had not interrupted the man before he could manage that.

Still, being thorough was his main attribute, and he went into the service porch and through into the kitchen.

That told him that his quarry had already been in the house, for the Frost kitchen was always both tidy and spotless. Now it showed signs of having been searched hastily, drawers pulled out, silverware disarranged, the papers on the work table shuffled and left scattered—Wash hoped intensely that neither of the Frosts had left any note concerning their intended destination. But Stony was no fool. He was pretty confident that had not happened. There was no point in going into the rest of the house. The man had been here. Now he was gone.

There was need to let Stony and Lily know, and to do that he would use a public phone on his way back to the office. Maybe that seemed paranoid, but when it came to Myron Duson, he felt nothing was too outrageous.

THE GUNS OF LIVINGSTON FROST

CHAPTER SIXTEEN

MYRON DUSON

His heart pounding, Duson rolled his waiting pickup out of the side road in which he had left it and switched on the engine. He had not thought he'd come back to it so quickly—and without accomplishing his goal. Getting into the house had been easy.

It was so big and rambling that searching it thoroughly was not feasible. It was clear that they were no longer living in the house, for he had checked the bedrooms upstairs, and they were empty. The kitchen desk had obviously been the center of business for the household, and among all the papers and ledgers there had been no indication of any intention to leave their home.

Damn that woman! She seemed to lead a charmed life. Why should someone be out at night, watching her house, when her attacker was supposed to be over in Louisiana, running away as fast as he could?

Duson was disturbed. He was not used to losing his cool and breaking his cover, as he had back there in the semi-darkness. That other man—he had known Duson was there. He was convinced of that. Yet Duson had not known until too late that there had been another man on the grounds at all. That, of course, meant the fellow shared the abilities Myron had used so successfully over the years. He knew when an enemy was near. He heard when there was no sound. He felt the presence of another through his pores and read his intentions unerringly.

So. If this man, police or deputy or whatever, had so much in common with Duson, he must also have more. He would know that his quarry would come back to finish the job left incomplete. And he *had* known, that was clear.

It meant that the night's exercise had been futile. The woman was not there at all. Moving her would make far more sense than staking out the place every night until someone returned. She and her gun-dealer lover or husband or whatever had gone away.

He felt a jolt inside, as the memory returned. That magazine in the old people's house! It contained a story about a woman with the same name. Perhaps a relative?

All his instincts said, "Yes, a relative!" He had memorized the name and the town, simply because it was his habit to be thorough, to leave nothing undone. Duson chuckled, as the pickup jounced along a dirt track that intersected, a few miles along, a farm to market road. This would take him to a highway. In time and with some study of his highway maps, the route would lead to the farm of Alison Frost Vernier.

An old woman and a crippled gun dealer could never hope to protect that woman from him. The thought of finishing his task filled him with warmth, and he drove along humming, tapping his fingers on the steering wheel in a rhythmic accompaniment to his untuneful voice.

THE GUNS OF LIVINGSTON FROST

CHAPTER SEVENTEEN

ALISON FROST VERNIER

She had not realized how much she'd missed having family about her, Alison decided. After Louis died, she had flung herself into her work with total commitment, so as to avoid self-pity and loneliness, and that had worked very well. Still, there was nothing like having your own kin about you, even if they sometimes were irritating. Lily, for instance, was not what Alison liked to think of as a true Frost woman. The timidity, that shrinking from strangers must, her great-aunt thought, be a direct result of her flirtation with the drug culture. A simple attack by a burglar shouldn't have had such a drastic effect.

More than anything else, she had heard about the ill effects of misuse of drugs; this persuaded her drugs were dangerous. All it would take was for a government to foster drug abuse among its citizens, and it could run them like robots, for they would be too afraid to resist.

The mere idea made her furious. To find her own niece so passive made her even more so. She was determined to bring Lily out of her present frame of mind if it required shock therapy.

Alison knew herself to have the capacity for that— Louis had often told her it was kind of God to make her so caring for people and animals, for otherwise she would have been too dangerous to live.

She mopped her forehead with the back of one wrist, pushing back the crisp white curls that insisted on straggling from beneath the net under which she confined them. The dogs milled about her feet, licking elbows, knees, and hands indiscriminately; that brought a smile, for she was a fool for her setters.

Lily and Stony were bringing in fresh hay for bedding behind the smaller of the two tractors. That boy looked better than he had when they arrived, Alison had to admit. He'd been pale and drawn then, but now his eyes were bright, and if his cheeks were not rosy, it was because his olive complexion didn't flush.

"Where you want this load?" he called, his tone cheerful.

"Take it into the middle run and put it into the boxes there. That's where the pregnant bitches have their litters. Then we'll go to the house and cool off a bit. For spring, it's getting mighty hot." She finished feeding the group in her pen, checked to see that the others in the long line of dog runs had eaten well, and turned toward the house.

Maggie had iced tea and sandwiches ready, as usual. Alison ate an early light lunch, after her labors in the kennels, for she began her day before dawn. Stony and his sister, without her asking or even hinting, had adapted to her schedule and joined her every morning, helping her to do the chores. That allowed Cephus, who would otherwise have been doing such work, to mend fences or mow pastures or tend the few choice head of Angus cattle that were a part of the Vernier spread.

It was a wonderful arrangement. Having someone who understood and appreciated music and art, with whom to talk politics and international affairs, was even better. Her mealtimes had become stimulating instead of mere pauses to fuel her body.

She had decided, without daring as yet to mention it to her kin, that she wanted them to visit her more often. However, she felt that it might be selfish to ask them to spend more time with one who was, after all, the contemporary of their own grandfather. Today, however, she decided to risk it.

The table was set with the green glass dishes and goblets, and that told her Maggie had determined it to be summer, whether or not the calendar officially declared it. Alison plopped into her chair and grinned at Stony, who had turned up his glass of iced tea and drained it.

"You know, Aunt Allie, it's wonderful to be outside doing things. I never knew how much I was missing. My folks seemed to think that because I was twisted I couldn't do anything physical at all."

Lily nodded. "And I was a girl, so they didn't want me to do anything but girl things. I like active work a lot better. Martin..."—she paused, as if astonished that she had mentioned his name.

"Martin just dived in and did things and he never minded if I went right along with him. But he thought I ought to be just as enthusiastic about hurting people as I was about loading logs or running a cotton picker."

Ah! That was a good sign. Alison poured more tea all around and said, "Your mother was raised to be a lady. Dratted nuisance, of course, and she deserved better. She had the makings of a real person, under all those layers of foolishness."

She passed the platter of sandwiches, noting the glance that Lily turned toward her brother. "It's not easy getting over a misguided childhood, but let me tell you it's worth it.

"My own mother thought she was going to make a lady out of me. But I was a Frost, and my grandmother was still alive to show me what a person ought to be. She'd tackle a bear and give it the first two bites."

Lily giggled, choked on a bite, and was thumped soundly on the back by Stony. The sound of their laughter filled Alison with a feeling of great well-being.

Maggie came soundlessly into the room and bent to whisper into her ear. The feeling of satisfaction popped like a bubble. Alison rose and followed Maggie out of the room to the telephone.

"Miz Vernier? This is Sheriff Shipp back in Nichayac County. I'm sorry to tell you, but Myron Duson was in Stony's house last night. That doesn't mean he found anything to guide him to you, but it won't hurt to be on guard, do you think?"

"Thank you, Sheriff," she said, her heart feeling cold in her chest. "We will keep an eye open and take precautions. Let us know if you learn anything more, will you?"

She returned to the table and took her place, and she knew her expression was telling Stony and Lily that trouble was in the wind.

THE GUNS OF LIVINGSTON FROST

CHAPTER EIGHTEEN

WASHINGTON SHIPP

Shipp made it back to his office in jig time. Amy was asleep on the cot in the back room, her cheeks rosy, her white hair rumpled. He shook her regretfully. She was old now, and needed her rest, but this was important.

"Get the Sheriff over in Calcasieu Parish, will you, Amy, just as soon as he's in his office? I need to make a run over there and check out that murder site. I'm missing something, I know, and I need to stand in that bastard's tracks and smell him out."

"What time is it?" She yawned, reached up to push several huge hairpins back into the braided snails of hair that covered each of her ears.

"Four-oh-five," he said.

The pot was plugged in, as usual, and he poured hot water into a Styrofoam cup and spooned in instant coffee. He was chilled to the bone, though the spring night was more damp than cold. Learning that his quarry had the same finely honed instincts he possessed was a worrying thing, and he thought that might have shaken him more than he knew.

Amy reached for the battered alarm clock sitting on the spindly chair beside the cot. "I'm setting it for six. You go home and get a little sleep, if you can, and as soon as I get word I'll call you at home," she told him.

"If I were your wife, I'd scrag you, Wash. I don't know how Jewel stands it. You're not at home any more than a tomcat."

He grinned at her, finishing his coffee. "But for very different reasons, Amy. Very different reasons."

He switched off the overhead light and left her to what remained of the night, but he didn't go home. Instead, he drove again to the Frost house, hidden behind its screen of hollies and crepe myrtles, crouching beneath its overgrown oaks and pines.

Using his torch, he moved around the silent building, examining the ground carefully for tracks. Duson had come in from the front and gone around to the kitchen door. Bold bastard! He must have hidden his car down the road, where a track led off into the woods, and walked back in the cover of the roadside undergrowth.

He went around the house on the north side, keeping close to the thick clumps of bridal wreath and camellias. Duson had emerged from the house not far from the holly under which Scott had hidden; he'd stood there for some time, still as a rock. The edges of his tracks weren't blurred with movement, but the prints themselves were well sunk into the damp soil, showing that he had been there for a while.

Just as he had been himself, Wash thought, like two jungle animals, each sensing the presence of the other, listening, feeling outward with every perception they had, trying to get the jump, when the time came, on the enemy who was perceived but not seen. He shivered hard, feeling again that raw moment of awareness.

The man had run north, pushing through the privet hedge and moving into the mixed hardwood and pine forest that formed the northern two acres of the Frost estate. He had reconnoitered the place well, Shipp figured, before the first break-in. Now he knew the best approach and the best retreat from this dark house.

It was becoming lighter in the east, the first pale streak lying along the horizon, where it could be seen between the big trees. There was dew thick on Shipp's windshield, and he turned on the wipers for a moment before backing out of the driveway, avoiding the big tree at its entrance.

Then he stopped, staring at the face of the house, just becoming visible in the light of dawn. It looked enigmatic, smug, like a cat that had caught its prey in the night. He could almost see the tail of a mouse hanging out of the rounded lips of the upper and lower porches.

Wash shook his head sharply. That was nonsense. The problem had come from outside that gloomy structure, and no Victorian house, no matter how dark and overburdened with heavy antique furniture, could cow Washington Shipp.

He wasn't entirely sure about Myron Duson.

THE GUNS OF LIVINGSTON FROST

CHAPTER NINETEEN

MYRON DUSON

Duson pulled into a motel before daylight and parked behind the office, so his battered pickup was invisible from the highway. He didn't think that lawman back there in Templeton had seen him or his vehicle either, but he refused to take chances on that. Driving by day was not smart, and he intended to sleep the daylight hours away and set off again at twilight.

The place where he stopped was so small it didn't qualify as a town at all. There was a big truck stop with attached café and garage, a grocery across the state highway, and the motel a mile down the road where the state road crossed a U.S. Highway heading north and south.

Trees surrounded the double line of cottages, coming right up to the doors. That gave concealment as he came and went, which was always good. He registered with a sleepy clerk, who probably could hardly recall his own name even when he was wide awake, and got himself under cover before early risers began driving to work. Tomorrow he would steal another vehicle and head for northern Louisiana and that big farm where the old woman lived.

If his quarry wasn't there...but he knew in his gut that

she would be, along with the crippled gun dealer.

THE GUNS OF LIVINGSTON FROST

CHAPTER TWENTY

WASHINGTON SHIPP

Shipp turned off toward Merryville and made the series of sharp angles that took him past the school and onto the farm road heading toward Ragley. The deputy who had met him near the river bridge was driving faster than seemed reasonable on the narrow road, and Wash stepped down on the gas to keep him in sight.

They turned sharply right and left, after going through a town even smaller than Merryville, and crossed the railroad. Beyond that the deputy slowed somewhat, and in a few more miles he braked to turn into a steep drive leading between overhanging bushes. It was still muddy, churned up by the passage of many vehicles.

His wheels spun a bit, but Wash gunned the Chevy up the slope and turned aside to park on the grass beside the deputy's car. Once he stood in front of the neat little house, he felt a sudden pang of regret.

Proud people had lived here, making work substitute for money. The ship-lap siding was freshly whitewashed, the tin roof shining with aluminum paint. Everything was clean, neat, orderly.

Though the front porch sagged beneath the weight of years, it was obviously often swept, where muddy shoes hadn't tracked their prints between steps and door. Pots of ferns sat along the sides and vines climbed from others that were hung from hooks screwed into the beams of the roof.

It was too like his own mother's house for comfort, Wash decided. He could almost see the tidy old lady who had last swept the porch and watered the plants, as he climbed the steps and opened the screen door.

Inside it was dark, in contrast to the bright day, and he paused, letting his eyes adjust. Then the feeling of familiarity was back. The Greek Revival furniture told him that at some point these people had been better off. Books and magazines lay in straight-edged stacks on the floor beside the two rocking chairs, and more magazines were arranged on a library table along one wall.

"Nothing here to show what happened," said the deputy. "The old folks was found out back, the woman killed with a rock, the man beaten and strangled. I think the killer must've come through the house, because there's an empty pie pan on the kitchen table and an empty milk jug by the refrigerator, but I can't see any sign he come in here. Sheriff Elkin couldn', either."

Shipp nodded, but that old instinct was alert, on the job, telling him that Duson had stood here, almost in this spot. He had looked around—several scattered magazines on the table should have been piled neatly like the books on the floor.

He moved to examine them. A copy of *Sports Afield* was lying on its crumpled back cover, and as he straightened it, almost hearing his mother's admonitions to be neat, it fell open at a photograph. Alison Frost Vernier.

He jerked, gripping the magazine. The deputy looked at him questioningly, and he asked, "Do you mind if I take this? I've got an ongoing case that this might work into. Or does Sheriff Elkin want everything kept just as it is?"

"I'll ask. You want to come out back with me? I think

he's out there again."

They went down a narrow hall, whose walls were tacked full of photographs of grandchildren and family gatherings, through the kitchen, and down the back steps. A worn mop hung from a hook in the door facing, just as his mother's always had.

Again he felt a surge of sadness. Why should decent people die at the hands of a mad dog like Duson?

Elkins was pacing off the distance from the edge of the yard, stalking toward a scuffed spot in the spring grass. He looked up and said, "You must be Sheriff Shipp from Templeton. Your dispatcher called to say you were comin'. You got something that ties into this?"

Shipp nodded. "We had a burglary and attempted murder over our way a couple of days ago. Got a description that matches up with the prints you found on the abandoned car up the road. I think Myron Duson is the man we both want.

"This magazine I found in the front room has an article about a woman that's kin to the victim of our crime. You mind if I take it? That's where the girl's gone, and if Duson saw this while he was here, it means he might know where to find her."

"Lord, man, take it! No magazine's going to help us catch that bastard. If you get him first, we want him. Better to hang a Murder One charge on him than anything less that he might get off on." Elkin wiped his pink forehead on his sleeve and stared back at the fence and its betraying loose strand of barbed wire.

"That's how he come. Left the road up a ways, come through the pasture, kicked loose the wire, and come up on the old folks from the back. The old lady was lyin' right there, and next to her was a rock with her blood and brains on it."

"Deputy Fuller says the old man was strangled," Wash said. "He must have heard something and come to see, you think?"

"You can see how his crutch is lyin'—I think he come at the killer tryin' to get him with the only weapon he had, but it's hard to say for sure. However it was, we want this bastard the worst way. Good luck with findin' him, Sheriff." Elkins turned as another deputy came around the house and signaled for his attention.

Wash glanced at the scuffed spot, whose upper end was stained with dried blood, and shivered. Sometimes he was almost glad his own folks were safely dead and out of this crazy world. They'd lived good lives, and a car accident wasn't the worst way to go, by any means.

"Thanks," he said. "I think I've got what I need."

Then he hurried to his car and headed back toward Texas. He had no authority in Louisiana, but once he made some calls from his office in Templeton, he thought he might get some people in Bossier Parish on the ball.

He couldn't afford to take the chance that Myron Duson hadn't found that betraying name in the magazine left so carelessly crumpled on the table in that pitiful house. It was all but certain, at least to him, that the folks who lived there would never in a million years have left one of their publications out of line, much less crumpled as it had been.

He sped along the blacktop road toward Merryville, his mind busy. What could he do to safeguard Stony and Lily and their very old great-aunt? That was the problem that plagued him as he headed for home.

THE GUNS OF LIVINGSTON FROST

CHAPTER TWENTY-ONE

MARTIN FEWELL

The ancient clunker rattled and left a trail of blue exhaust as it moved, but it did move, and that was all Martin had expected of it. More, in fact. It wouldn't have surprised him if the pickup had died on him before he passed Jasper. But it coughed and wheezed its way into Templeton and let out its last gasp in front of a junkyard, which Fewell thought provided a nice, ironic touch.

The fellow in the junkyard didn't ask for proof of ownership, though if Martin recalled his Texas law correctly he probably should have. He paid fifty bucks for the thing, and Martin felt himself lucky to get that much.

It might be a tad illegal, but that bastard who'd taken his own truck was still moving, and he had to have some traveling money. What was in his pocket was, as always, pretty skimpy.

Templeton hadn't changed much in the years since he'd shaken the dust off his feet and taken Lily Frost away from her protesting family. Little towns like that one never had enough industry to bring in money to make changes, he knew. He avoided the side street leading past the combined police station and jail, crossed the intersecting highway that went north and south, and found the country road that went to the Frost place. His feet knew the way, though he had always driven it in his psychedelically painted van, back in the old days.

It was a damn long walk, and it was getting pretty dark before he found the big tree sticking out into the road that marked the Frost drive. He'd always wondered why they didn't cut the thing down, and all Lily's explanations never convinced him that any tree, however old and historical, was worth a minute of his time or an iota of inconvenience.

Now he was grateful for its nine-foot-thick trunk. The bushes had grown a lot, and he might have missed the drive altogether without it.

He checked the road before darting into the concealment of the crepe myrtles. The last sunset light did nothing to make his way easier as he crept along the front porch, heading for the rear of the house. He'd never been in the front door, a matter of some bitterness at the time, but he intended to go the way he knew.

If Lily and her crip brother were there, he wanted to make sure they were all right. He wasn't certain if he intended for them to know he was checking on them.

He had a funny feeling about what he was doing, anyway. Never in his life had he done anything just to help someone, and it felt strange.

Once he got to the back of the house, he realized that it was too quiet. No light shone through any window, though there was a dim glow from the store room. The kitchen was dark behind the low overhang of the back porch. They were gone. That was good thinking. But somehow he felt that the danger wasn't altogether averted. There was still a chill in his backbone that told him someone was about.

It was now very dark. The idea of walking back to town and spending some of his scanty cash on a room wasn't inviting. Besides, he had a feeling something might well happen before the night was over.

Here was an empty house, and he had learned to pick locks while he was in prison. Before the last light left the sky he was inside. It smelled old, that house, but not the kind of old Martin Fewell understood. This was a rich, mellow sort of scent, compounded of leather and furniture polish, candles, and the acrid smell of cold fireplaces.

The kitchen was recognizable the instant he stuck his head in at the door. Generations of rich food seemed to linger in the air, along with the lemony smell of dish detergent.

He didn't turn on a light—who knew what sorts of neighbors might be able to see it and call the cops?—but his skilled, silent fingers checked out a cupboard that held crackers and canned meat. A swift search found a can opener, and he ate standing at the sink. Uncharacteristically, he rinsed out the can and swilled out the sink before turning to go over the rest of the house. Martin had a sheepish feeling about Lily's knowing he had been prying into her kitchen. He had treated her too badly to expect forgiveness; he didn't think he could face her anger.

He crept through the still rooms, smelling the scent of wax and polish and old books. Something drew him to an upstairs window, at last, to look down on the dark lawn.

The blackness inside the house made the outside almost visible, the grass gray, the clumps of shrubbery dense shadows. As he looked down, one blot of darkness moved away from another much larger one. A man was creeping over the grass. He moved into the shadow of the crepe myrtles along the walk; before Martin could decide what to make of that, another figure moved away from the same shelter.

Two men had been watching the house. One had to be the man who'd tried to kill Lily, but who had the other one been? The law? Possibly, but Fewell had no intention of depending on that.

He watched until the second shadow was out of sight.

He waited until the clock with the loud tick, which had been noting the half-hour with a light chime, cleared its throat and bonged once. Time to go. There would be no sleep for him tonight, for he knew he must search the house until he found some indication of Lily's whereabouts. He had seen from the state of the kitchen that someone had been there before him, and he hoped nothing had been there to tell where the family had gone.

Whether she and her brother knew it or not, they needed someone to keep watch over them, and Martin Fewell knew that was his job. He'd earned it the hard way, just as he had earned his belated conscience.

Hurting Lily had been the thing he did best. Now he had to make certain that nobody else took up that task.

THE GUNS OF LIVINGSTON FROST

CHAPTER TWENTY-TWO

WASHINGTON SHIPP

Shipp pulled into town in mid-afternoon and stopped by the office to see if anything had come in that needed his attention. It was the family's night. He always took Jewel and the boy to visit Jewel's parents or else to the art museum or the zoo. They both believed in exposing their small son to a wide range of experiences.

Amy had a pile of stuff on his desk, and he went through it carefully, signing letters, checking out reports, noting anything unusual. Before he was through, Amy tapped at his door.

"You've got a call from Ned Tubbs at the junk yard. He got in a dead pickup this afternoon, and the fellow seemed to be in a terrible hurry. Ned fudged on ownership papers, as the thing was good for nothing but scrap metal, but now he wants to talk to you about it."

Wash could tell that she was afire with curiosity, for Ned avoided the law as if he were a hardened criminal. Yet in all the years he'd had his junkyard, Shipp had never caught him doing anything illegal. "I'll take it," he said. "Close the door, Amy."

With a sniff, she went out, the door snapping shut behind her with an irritable click. Shipp lifted the phone and said, "Ned? What you got on your mind, man?"

There was a short silence. Then Ned coughed and snorted, as usual, before speaking. "I had the radio on but I wasn't listenin' close. Then I caught a story about a old couple over in Louisiana that got killed and their pickup was stole. Well, yesterday afternoon I taken in a junker with Louisiana tags. I went out and looked, and sure enough, they match up with the ones the feller on the radio said. At least I think they do. You better come out and look, Sheriff." Better mark that on the calendar as a red letter day, Shipp thought. The day Ned Tubbs actually invited the sheriff out to his place.

"Be right out, Ned," he said. "Don't you touch the thing any more than you can help. If it's the one, we may get prints off it. Don't let Teebo mess with it, you hear? That boy just likes to get his hands on any kind of vehicle, whether it runs or not."

Ned chuckled. "He's a borned mechanic, I got to say. But I'll warn him off. I don't think he touched it yet—he's been guttin' a big Caddy that come in last week with its side bashed in."

Wash cradled the phone and shrugged on his jacket again. It might be dark by the time he finished. Too late for the family outing, he was sure.

"Amy!" He stuck his head out into the hallway. "Can you call my wife and tell her that I won't be home till late? Tell her I'll take her and the boy someplace tomorrow, if I can. I'm going out to Ned's."

* * * * * * *

The junk yard was a treasury of rusty refrigerators, remnants of automobiles, wagon wheels, hoe-heads, and rakes without handles, not to mention every other sort of throwaway possible to imagine. Everything was sorted with painful neatness, each kind to itself, in rows or piles or whatever arrangement its anatomy dictated.

Shipp pulled up inside the chain link fence, whose utilitarian skeleton was veiled by yellow jasmine vines most of the year. Already there were fragrant golden bells among the dark green foliage.

He honked once. Ned waddled out, his round shape all but lost in overalls large enough to contain two of him. "Over here, Sheriff," he called, pointing to the part of the yard devoted to the corpses of cars and trucks.

Wash approached the dilapidated truck with hope and doubt. It would be too much luck to have that pickup turn up here in his own front yard. Yet Duson had been at the Frost house last night—who else would have been hiding in the myrtles, checking out the place? He could easily have driven the distance by yesterday afternoon.

The plates were a match. Somehow he'd known they would be. The description was dead on.

"Good work, Ned. I can understand your not making a fuss about papers on this clunker, but I sure am glad you heard that newscast. This is the very truck Duson stole."

He had brought a plastic tarp, and with Ned's help he tied it over the truck to help preserve any prints or dust or other data that the specialists might pick up tomorrow. Then he rummaged in his wallet and pulled out a photocopy of a mug shot. "Is this the man who sold it?"

The sun was down, and chilly darkness was creeping among the orderly rows of junk. "Cain't see very good," Ned said, squinting at the picture. "Come over here to the office, and I'll take a gander at it."

The light in the office was all of forty watts, but it seemed enough. Ned took one glance and shook his head. "It's kind of like him, but it's not the same man. The one that sold the truck was a lot skinnier, face thinner, wrinkled like a turtle. He looked tired, not mean. This fella's younger and looks a hell of a lot meaner."

Shipp looked at him in surprise. "You dead certain of

that? This is a picture of Duson that was made the last time he was arrested. He might have lost weight."

Ned held the photo closer to his face. He turned it sideways, upside down, back right side up. He shook his head again. "No way this is the same man. Same type, yes. Head's shaped some the same. But the face is wrong. The eyes are different. The chin is sharper. Just ain't the same man, Sheriff, and that's all I can say."

"Then who in hell...?" Shipp chopped off his words and sighed. "Thanks, Ned. I'll sort this out some way, but damned if I know how, just yet. There'll be a man out in the morning to check for fingerprints and take samples. You'll be here?"

"Every day 'cept Sunday, Sheriff. You just tell him to blow three times, so I'll know it ain't Teebo, and I'll be out like a shot. You think you'll ketch that bastard?"

"I hope so. I certainly hope so. Thanks again, Ned. And good night."

THE GUNS OF LIVINGSTON FROST

CHAPTER TWENTY-THREE

MARTIN FEWELL

Martin had searched the house thoroughly. Not once but twice he had gone through the place; every nook and cranny (and there had been more than he cared to think about) had been explored, without result. Weary and dusty, he retired to the kitchen, where he fixed a cup of hot broth from a packet of dry mix he found in a cupboard.

Deciding at last that it was safe to turn on a light, after pulling the old fashioned green shades over the windows, he switched on the lamp sitting on the little desk in the corner. The big kitchen seemed to be a sort of living room, and evidently Frost or Lily did household bookkeeping at the desk.

He searched it again, without much hope, and this time he found a twist of paper tucked back in the corner of a drawer. He smoothed it out, and there he found a phone number. Beside it were two words: Aunt Alison.

The area code was 318, and he rummaged out the phone book and found that number. The western half of Louisiana. Without much hope, he called Information and asked in what city the number would be located. To his surprise, there was no question, just a swift reply.

He tucked the note into his pocket, glanced around to

make certain there was no sign of his intrusion into the kitchen, and slid out of the back door, re-locking it behind him. He'd get to Bossier City hitch-hiking, if necessary, and then he could walk up to Plain Dealing, if he had to.

A phone call by day might get him some directions. He could pretend to be some sort of repair man or maybe somebody about the fire insurance on the house. Everybody had that, and it had always put him where he wanted to be.

He had recognized that name, Alison. Lily Frost had two living relatives, one her brother Livingston, the other her grandfather's sister, whose name was Alison Vernier. Martin never forgot anything that might be useful, and that had been important information, in case Lily ever escaped from him. In the old days he would have run her down and beaten anybody to a pulp who offered to interfere. Now his purpose was different.

Where would the Frosts have gone, except to kin? They had to be there, and he had to go too. It was his job to make up for past sins, and keeping Lily safe was more important than anything else. Since he'd heard about Duson's attack on her, his world had shrunk to that single focus.

He hoped to deal with Duson, in time, but first he had to safeguard Lily. Thinking about what he would do to her attacker would keep him warm all night.

In pitch darkness, he trudged away up the oil-top road, keeping himself oriented by the distant band of stars above the flanking treetops. His small bundle of newly acquired underwear seemed heavy, and he was older than he used to be, but he didn't let either slow his steps. He'd get to Bossier City if he had to crawl.

As it turned out, a freelance trucker with a load of heifers for a farmer in Tennessee picked him up on the highway before he'd walked more than a dozen miles. The fellow was sleepy, for he'd been driving all night, and he needed somebody to keep him awake.

In the old days, Martin thought wryly, nobody in his right mind would have picked him up, because he used to be so big and tough and mean-looking. Now he only looked weary, as he had noted in Lily's mirror: no threat to anyone. He was so thin and stooped that he didn't even seem big any more. He talked randomly about all sorts of things as they bored through the night toward Shreveport. When they hit the Interstate west of Shreveport, he ran out of talk, and besides it was time to change off. It never paid to stick too long with one ride, even when you were going to do something honest.

"If you can let me off close to the airport, that'd be real nice," he said.

The man nodded, wakeful now that daylight had come and there was enough traffic to keep him alert. "Will do. Been nice to hear your stories. I never got to travel. Just covered ground with the truck loaded and come back empty, like a yo-yo on a string. You okay for cash?"

Martin was startled. He'd forgotten, in all his years of muscle work and con-games, that people sometimes cared to help each other.

"I'll be fine," he said. "Got an old aunt lives close to the airport, and that's where I'm goin'. Much obliged for the ride. Helped me out a lot."

He watched the rig pull away into the rising sun. Then he headed for Bossier on foot, using streets he remembered from his youth.

He'd actually had an aunt, once, who lived somewhere near this place. Things had changed, even in the few years since he'd come this way, but he knew where he was going and how to get there.

THE GUNS OF LIVINGSTON FROST

CHAPTER TWENTY-FOUR

WASHINGTON SHIPP

The sheriff had dreamed about that pickup. He was out at the junk yard as soon as he'd checked the office and done the few major jobs waiting for him. Following him in a shiny van was Phil Taylor, on loan from the state, who had the equipment to examine the truck from stem to stern.

"If there's a hair or a print or even a grain of dust there, I'll find it," he promised, as he approached the plastic-veiled vehicle. "As it's crossed the state line, the Feds may be interested too. I'll keep you posted, Sheriff."

Wash nodded as he backed out of the drive and headed back toward town. He had a feeling about that truck. If the driver wasn't Duson, who in hell could it be? With the impact of inspiration, he had an idea that propelled him toward his office with the sort of speed he often chided his deputies for using.

Lily had thought Duson was Martin Fewell, when he came into her kitchen. There had to be some resemblance between them.

Ned said Duson's picture was similar to the man he'd seen, but definitely not the same person. Could, somehow, Martin Fewell have reentered the field? How? Why? For what reason? There was only one way to find out.

He entered the building in an uncharacteristic rush and leaned over the desk where Amy worked. "Amy, call Miz Vernier, will you? I need to talk to Lily," he said. "I'll be in my office."

When the call came through he was staring at his file cabinet as if to burn a hole in its gray-painted side. Something was bugging him, and he wasn't quite able to pin it down.

"Lily? Hi, there. Yes, things seem pretty quiet here, too. Listen, do you have a picture of Martin Fewell? I mean, here at the house where I might use the key you left to pick it up?"

"Why, no, Wash," she said. "I think I burned them all. But wouldn't you have one someplace in your files? He was wanted for quite a few years before they sent him up." She sounded worried, and he knew that old fear must be chipping away at her new-found balance.

"Now why didn't I think of that? Of course—there ought to be something in the books. He was arrested here at least once, and if not, I can get a picture out of the morgue at the paper. Thanks, Lily-bird. You and Stony keep your noses clean, you hear?"

"Aunt Alison is carrying her pistol in her pocket. She may be ninety, but she'll take care of us if it kills her." To his relief there was a hint of laughter in her voice.

He rummaged in the back files for the year when Fewell had run afoul of the law in Nichayac County. It wasn't all that far back, and he soon had the thin sheaf of paperwork in hand. There was a mug shot, but it didn't even look like the Fewell that Shipp had known at the time.

It took all morning to find a news photo that looked anything like the man. But he located one at last in the dusty files of the *Courier* and had Sue-Ann, the reporter-cum dogbody there, run him a photocopy that was passable. Then he headed back for the junk yard.

When he handed Ned the punched-up photo copy, the junk dealer nodded. "Yep, that's him. A bit younger and not so tired and skinny, but that's the man."

Something inside Wash resonated to his words. Somehow he had known that Fewell was going to come back into the picture, and here he was. But how did he fit? Was he acquainted with Myron Duson? Were they in cahoots?

It might be that Lily Frost would know. Her lover might have talked about his convict friends, and they had been in the same penitentiary for at least a couple of years that overlapped. His investigations into Duson's career had told him that.

Wash returned to his office and dropped into his chair absentmindedly. He had no authority in Bossier Parish. The sheriff there was an unknown quantity. Going himself would be officious and his Louisiana counterpart would make that clear, he was certain.

However, it might have been Fewell instead of Duson under that bush at the Frost house that night. And if so, he might have picked up some clue as to the whereabouts of the Frosts.

That same instinct told him that Alison Vernier's farm wasn't going to be as secure a hideout as they had all thought, but he had no proof, not even a real clue. How did you tell a skeptical official you'd never met that you have a hunch there's going to be trouble in his vicinity?

"With great difficulty," he replied to himself. Then he dialed the Vernier number himself, not wanting Amy to be a witness to his humiliation.

THE GUNS OF LIVINGSTON FROST

CHAPTER TWENTY-FIVE

MYRON DUSON

The new roads up the country made Duson's trip much shorter than it would have been in the days when the highways seemed to go right through every pea-turkey little town and around their squares twice. Duson had lifted a nice little Toyota in San Augustine; it was parked behind a gas station just waiting for its owner to show up after having it serviced and gassed. Now he whizzed along through the pine woods, noting the thin screens of standing timber that hid the devastation of loggers behind their scanty ranks.

He'd robbed a few loggers in his time, but they never had anything but grease and sweat on them. It had always puzzled Duson why anybody would work so hard for so little, when it was so easy to take what others sweated to earn. But he guessed it took all kinds, which made it nice for him. There wasn't all that much competition in his trade, and his stints in the slammer hadn't been all that bad. He'd made contacts, though the way this last job had turned out, he was about to decide that the quality of convicts was going down. It wasn't easy to get good help, and that was a fact. The idiots couldn't even hit a woman over the head and kill her, any more.

After a while he pulled over into a rest stop and studied his road map. Plain Dealing...it was a dinky little place, but not hard to find, and very close to Shreveport.

As it was about time to change cars again, he waited, hiding behind a picnic table, until a couple pulled up in a newish Ford and headed, both at the same time, for the rest rooms. All you had to do was wait, he'd always known.

He sighed. At last things were going right again. He jiggered the lock with his special device and hot-wired the ignition in less time than he could have done the job with the keys. He slid out of the park and into traffic, already looking for the turnoff he wanted.

Once he was headed for Plain Dealing, he got cautious and took back roads, blessing his long experience with dodging the law in these parts. To his surprise, he passed two county cars on the way, both driven by men who seemed to be watching for somebody.

He'd changed vehicles just in time, he realized. Probably was some local problem that had them stirred up like a nest of hornets.

THE GUNS OF LIVINGSTON FROST

CONCLUSION

Summary of ending:

Now Myron Duson is heading for the Vernier farm in Louisiana. So is Martin Fewell on foot, and Washington Shipp has alerted the local sheriff to the potential danger facing the Frosts. Deputies are on their way.

Alison is armed, as is Stony, and Lily has gained enough confidence to defend herself as well. They all will come together in an explosive encounter, which will leave an astonished Myron Duson wounded and in custody and poor Martin Fewell dead. However, the Frosts survive and return to their lives, both sister and brother now assured of care and affection from each other and their aged aunt.

ABOUT THE AUTHOR

The author of seventy books, more than forty of them published commercially, **ARDATH MAYHAR** began her career in the early eighties with science fiction novels from Doubleday and TSR. Atheneum published several of her young adult and children's novels. Changing focus, she wrote westerns (as **Frank Cannon**) and mountain man novels (as **John Killdeer**), four prehistoric Indian books under her own name, and historical western *High Mountain Winter* under the byline **Frances Hurst**.

Recently she has been working with on-line publishers. *A Road of Stars* was her first original novel to appear in print-on-demand format. Many of her out-of-print titles are now available from e-publishers fictionwise.com and renebooks.com; many other novels are being published by the Borgo Press Imprint of Wildside Press.

Now eighty, Mayhar was widowed in 1999, after forty-one years of marriage, and has four grown sons. She works at home, writing short fiction and nonfiction, and doing book doctoring professionally. Her web pages can be found at:

w2.netdot.com/ardathm/

and

http://ofearna.us/books/mayhar.html

www.ingramcontent.com/pod-product-compliance
Lightning Source LLC
Chambersburg PA
CBHW050737250626
47155CB00005B/1811